SURROUNDED!

Clint moved quickly, dropping to his knees and grabbing one of the fallen guns.... He came up with the gun and began to fire as quickly as he could thumb back the hammer on the single-action Colt....

The gun in Clint's hand was suddenly empty, and he tossed it aside and picked up the Emperor's Sword. In a split second he was side by side with Matsu, and their blades were flashing and hacking....

DON'T MISS THESE
ALL-ACTION WESTERN SERIES
FROM THE BERKLEY PUBLISHING GROUP

THE GUNSMITH by J.R. Roberts
Clint Adams was a legend among lawmen, outlaws, and ladies. They called him . . . the Gunsmith.

LONGARM by Tabor Evans
The popular long-running series about U.S. Deputy Marshal Long—his life, his loves, his fight for justice.

LONE STAR by Wesley Ellis
The blazing adventures of Jessica Starbuck and the martial arts master, Ki. Over eight million copies in print.

SLOCUM by Jake Logan
Today's longest-running action western. John Slocum rides a deadly trail of hot blood and cold steel.

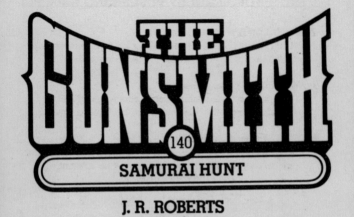

THE GUNSMITH

140

SAMURAI HUNT

J. R. ROBERTS

JOVE BOOKS, NEW YORK

SAMURAI HUNT

A Jove Book / published by arrangement with
the author

PRINTING HISTORY
Jove edition / August 1993

All rights reserved.
Copyright © 1993 by Robert J. Randisi.
This book may not be reproduced in whole
or in part, by mimeograph or any other means,
without permission. For information address:
The Berkley Publishing Group, 200 Madison Avenue,
New York, New York 10016.

ISBN: 0-515-11168-6

Jove Books are published by The Berkley Publishing Group,
200 Madison Avenue, New York, New York 10016.
The name "JOVE" and the "J" logo
are trademarks belonging to Jove Publications, Inc.

PRINTED IN THE UNITED STATES OF AMERICA

10 9 8 7 6 5 4 3 2 1

THE GUNSMITH

140

SAMURAI HUNT

ONE

Lately Clint Adams found himself spending much of his time in one of two places. He was either in Labyrinth, Texas, or in San Francisco. Over the years he'd traveled to almost every major city in the United States, as well as to South America, Europe, and Australia. With all that traveling under his belt he had picked out his two favorite places in the world with considerable ease.

When he wanted some quiet time he'd go to Labyrinth to visit with his friend Rick Hartman, who ran a saloon and gambling house called Rick's Place. Rick did not, however, offer much more in the way of gambling than poker, faro, and roulette, and the poker game tended to be on a somewhat small scale.

When Clint wanted some heavy action—"action" as in cards *and* women—he went to San Francisco, or sometimes to Sacramento. On this particular occasion, it was San Francisco. He was staying in a small hotel just off Portsmouth

Square, where all the major gambling houses were.

He tried not to stay in the same hotel each time he went to San Francisco. A man with his reputation couldn't afford to set up a recognizable pattern of behavior. He also didn't gamble in the same casino each night, unless it was at an organized poker game in one of the private rooms. If that was the case, there was always a security force available to watch his back—as well as the backs of the other players.

Clint was staying in a small but fairly elegant hotel called The Clapton House. The owner was a man named Elton Clapton, who was never seen on the premises. He left the running of the hotel to his manager, Peter Styles.

Clint had met Styles during previous visits to San Francisco but had never before stayed at The Clapton House. He had decided that on this trip he would give it a try. Upon his arrival Styles had made him feel very welcome, giving him one of the best rooms in the hotel.

Styles was also a poker player, which was how he and Clint had met in the past. They had never socialized away from the tables, and it was only during Clint's stay at the hotel that the two men had had any lengthy conversations. They had fallen into an attitude of easy comraderie, as if they had been friends for a long time.

Clint had been staying there for a week when he came down for breakfast and saw Styles sitting at his private table in a corner of the dining room. As Clint entered the dining room, the hotel manager saw him and beckoned him over with his fork. When Clint walked over, Styles said, "Join me for breakfast."

"Who's buying?" Clint asked.

"The House," Styles said, with a smile.

Peter Styles was young, in his early forties, with very black hair that had yet to show any gray. He was tall, over six feet, square shouldered and square jawed. He was popular with the ladies, which was something else the two men had in common. Being around the well-dressed Styles, however, always made Clint feel like an unmade bed. The man's black hair and equally black beard were always impeccably trimmed.

The waiter came over and asked Clint what he would like for breakfast. He was a small, white-haired man in his sixties named Felix, who had served Clint every time he had dined there.

"The usual, Felix," Clint said.

"Of course, sir," Felix said. He bowed to both men and backed away from the table.

"Got my staff trained already, I see?" Styles asked.

"I'm working on it," Clint said. "Before I leave I should have this place whipped into almost working order."

"Oh-ho," Styles said, "this is the best run hotel in San Francisco, and you know it."

"Yes," Clint said seriously, "I do know it. You know, I heard last night—quite by accident, that is—that you turned down an offer to run the Alhambra."

Styles didn't look up from his plate.

"The *Alhambra*, Peter?"

Styles shrugged. "I like it here, Clint."

"Yeah, Peter," Clint said, "but the *Alhambra*!" He had learned long ago, even before they had become friends, that no one called Styles "Pete." It was always "Peter."

Very carefully Styles set down his knife and fork and looked up from his steak and eggs.

"I owe Mr. Clapton a lot, Clint," he said slowly. "It would not be fair, or loyal, of me to leave him just because the Alhambra is a bigger operation."

"Did you discuss it with him?"

"Of course not," Styles said. "It's my decision, not his."

"Don't you think he would tell you to go, Peter?" Clint asked.

"That's beside the point, Clint," Styles said, picking up his knife and fork again. "You of all people should understand loyalty."

"I do understand it," Clint said. "I just hope I can one day do the word as much justice as you're doing it."

Styles waved the compliment away as if it were an annoying insect buzzing around his head. Felix came with Clint's breakfast, and the two men ate in silence for a short while before Styles spoke again.

"I'm sorry," he said.

"About what?"

"About being so touchy."

"Hey, you're entitled," Clint said. "Obviously, I don't know all of the details of your relationship with Mr. Clapton."

"No, you don't."

"That's fine, then," Clint said. "You have nothing to explain to me, and nothing to apologize for."

"Well . . . good," Styles said.

"Now finish your breakfast," Clint said. "You'll insult the cook if you don't. He's very sensitive."

Styles stared at Clint. "You even know *that*?"

"Hey," Clint said, "if a man prepares my food, I like to make sure I get to know him."

TWO

Toshiro Matsu was in a strange place. The people walking around him, staring at him, were strangely dressed. As he walked along the dock, his meager belongings wrapped in a silk cloth and carried in one hand, he began to realize that it was not they who were strange, but he. This place, this United States—specifically San Francisco— was very different from his homeland of Japan.

All the men around him wore guns. He wore his *katana* on his back, where it was easily accessible by reaching over either shoulder with his right hand. The sword, he realized, would be utterly useless against a gun, unless he were within striking distance. Luckily his quarries were not men who carried guns, but men like himself, his countrymen. Except they had become traitors to their Emperor.

It was in the service of his Emperor that Matsu was here. He hoped to find the men he sought quickly, reclaim what they had stolen and return to his homeland as soon as possible.

He did not like this strange land.

6

THREE

"Okay," Peter Styles said over coffee, "maybe you deserve an explanation."

Clint looked across the table, bewildered. "I didn't say anything."

"I know you didn't," Styles said, "but you're thinking it."

"Thinking what?"

"How can I turn down an offer from one of the biggest houses in San Francisco?"

"That's your business, Peter."

"Yes, I know," Styles said, "but I want to tell it, okay?"

"That's different," Clint said, glad that his curiosity was going to be satisfied. "If you want to tell it, I'll be only too happy to listen."

"Well," Styles said, shifting uncomfortably in his seat, "there's not all that much to tell, really. I've run big houses like that—well, maybe not as big as the Alhambra, but certainly bigger than The Clapton House. I did it for years, run them *and* worked in them, and you know what?"

After a pause, Clint asked, "What?"

"I don't like the people."

"The people who worked with you," Clint asked, "or for you?"

"Neither," Styles said. "The people who *go* to those places. The rich people. The *gentry*." He said "gentry" as if it were a dirty word. "The society types, the bankers, the lawyers, the movers and shakers in the city who think you have to bend over backwards for them. You know what my favorite job was? Besides this, that is?"

"What?"

"I ran a small hotel and casino down on the Barbary Coast."

Clint tried to imagine the well-manicured Styles down on the docks.

"Really?"

"I don't look the type, right?"

"Well—"

"I tell you," Styles said, "you could take almost anybody off the Coast, cut their hair, give them a manicure and a clean set of clothes, and they'd fit in here. Let me tell you, it doesn't work the other way around."

Clint sat back for a moment, then said, "I can see what you mean."

"Can you?"

Clint nodded.

"I've been around both kinds of people enough to know which ones are the most honest," he said.

Styles laughed. "Honest? I don't think the word really applies to either group."

"I don't mean *that* kind of honest," Clint said.

"I mean which of them is the least phony. Generally, if you walk into a Barbary Coast saloon, what you see is what you get. Nobody's trying to be something they're not."

Styles thought a moment, rubbing his jaw. "I see what you mean. I guess that's what I really don't like about the big houses. Now this—" he spread his arms to indicate the hotel they were in, "this is halfway between the two."

"How long have you been running this hotel?" Clint asked.

"Ever since Mr. Clapton bought it two years ago," Styles said. "He came to me before he bought it and asked if I'd run it for him. I told him I would, so he bought it. You should have seen it when I took it over. It was in bad shape, and half the rooms were empty. Now we're filled to capacity every week."

"You know your job," Clint said.

"Oh, yes," Styles responded. "I know what I'm doing when it comes to running a hotel. I put just enough gaming tables in the saloon to make a difference, you know? And a couple of girls to work the room, but *not* the customers. If men want *that* they can go to the Barbary Coast."

"Right," Clint said, averting Styles's eyes. He wondered if the manager knew that he had been bedding one of the girls who worked at the hotel, a dark-haired, slender beauty named Karen.

"All right," Styles said, "so now you know enough. . . ."

Obviously, there was more to know, but Peter Styles wasn't going to talk about it any further—not then, anyway.

"Time to get to work," the hotel manager said and stood up. He moved quite well for a man who had one real foot, and one made of wood.

But that was another story.

FOUR

Toshiro Matsu walked into the Wayfarer Hotel near the docks and stopped at the desk. The sleepy clerk opened his eyes, took one look and then stared.

"I desire lodgings," Matsu said in heavily accented English. When the Emperor had asked him to make this journey, the man had taken an intense course in the language. He was considered, in his country, to be one who spoke it quite well.

However, to the clerk Matsu sounded as if he were asking for "rodgings."

"Huh?"

Matsu stopped, thought a moment, then nodded with satisfaction when he was able to pull another word out of his English vocabulary.

"A room," he said, "I desire—I *need* a room."

"Oh, uh, sure," the clerk said. "Can you, uh, sign the register?"

Matsu stared at the book, which the clerk had turned toward him. There was writing on it, but he could read no part of it.

"Not in English," he said to the clerk.

It sounded like "engrish."

"Uh, what's your name?" the clerk asked. "I'll write it for you."

"Matsu."

"Huh?"

"Matsu," Matsu said, and between them they managed to formulate an English spelling.

Matsu looked at his name written in English, ran his finger along it and said, "Ma-tsu," with a nod.

"Where are you from?" the clerk asked.

"Japan."

The clerk wrote J-a-p-a-n.

"Have you seen others from Japan?" Matsu asked.

"Uh," the clerk said, "no . . . I haven't." He turned away, grabbed a key and handed it to the Japanese man. "Room four. Up the stairs and on the right. Uh, this way," he added, pointing.

"The right," Matsu said, accepting the key.

"That's right," the clerk said. "The right."

Matsu nodded and said, *"Hai!"*

"What?"

Matsu frowned, then brightened and said, "Thank you."

"Oh, yeah, sure, you're welcome."

Matsu picked up his belongings and turned away. The clerk stared at the sword on the man's back as Matsu climbed the stairs. When the Japanese man was out of sight, the clerk hurried from around the desk and ran out the front door.

FIVE

Daryl Gaines looked up in annoyance as his secretary opened the door to his office. "I thought I told you I didn't want to be disturbed."

"I'm sorry, Mr. Gaines, but that man—the clerk from that hotel—is here."

"Clegg?"

She wrinkled her pretty nose and said, "Yes."

Gaines frowned.

"All right," he said, "let him in."

"Yes, sir."

Gaines stood up and walked over to the door. As Clegg came walking in, Gaines met the man with a vicious backhand blow. Even though Clegg was the larger of the two men, the blow rocked him; it never occurred to Clegg that he might strike back.

Clegg put his hand to his mouth, but before he could speak Gaines asked, "What the hell are you doing here?"

"It was important, Mr. Gaines."

"Close the door!"

As Clegg shut the door Gaines moved back

behind his desk. He shot his cuffs, adjusted his jacket and sat down.

"What is it, then?"

"Another one of them fellers showed up at the hotel," Clegg replied.

"Another one of *what* fellows?" Gaines asked.

"You know," Clegg said, and then lowered his voice. "Those funny Chinee."

"*Japanese*?" Gaines asked.

"Yeah, that's it," Clegg said. "One of them."

"He checked into the hotel?"

"Yessir."

Gaines frowned. "That's got to be a coincidence."

"That another Japanese is here in San Francisco?" Clegg asked.

"No, fool," Gaines said. "He's obviously here looking for the other two. No, it's got to be a coincidence that he came to your hotel. He can't know that the other two stayed there."

"Well, I didn't tell him."

"It's good for you that you didn't," Gaines said. "Did he ask?"

"Well . . . he asked if I'd seen any others like him."

"And you said?"

"No," Clegg answered quickly. "I said no, of course."

"Of course."

"He had one of them swords, like the other two," Clegg continued. "That's weird, ya know? I mean, who would rather carry one of them than a gun?"

"You wouldn't understand," said Gaines. "Is there anything else?"

"Uh, no," Clegg replied, "no, there ain't. I, uh, just thought you oughtta know right away."

"All right," Gaines said, "all right, then, you can go."

"Yessir."

As Clegg started for the door Gaines said, "Not that way. Take the back stairs."

"Yessir."

Clegg slunk out the other door. When the door had closed behind him, Gaines sat back in his chair to consider what to do next.

The other two Japanese would be leaving the next morning for Nevada, to deliver the sword to Gaines's client, the wealthy Mr. Henderson Burke. They would be taking the sword directly to Burke's ranch. It wouldn't be hard for this third Japanese to find out about the first two. Obviously, he had to be some kind of lawman, or bounty hunter, sent here to hunt down the two thieves and retrieve the sword.

Well, he was going to find out how dangerous it was to leave your homeland and come to a strange place.

He stood up, walked to the door of his office and opened it.

"Miss Bonner?"

"Yes, sir?"

As she turned toward him Gaines stopped, as he always did, to admire her. She was a lousy secretary, but she was good in bed, whereas his wife wasn't interested in sex at all. She was tall, and although slender, quite full breasted—and she was young. Gaines was thirty-five, and Miss Althea Bonner was a tender twenty-two. In the office he referred to her as "Miss Bonner" and she to him as "Mr. Gaines."

"I need Ballard," he said finally. "Get him here for me."

"Today?"

He closed his eyes. If she wasn't so damned good in bed . . .

"Yes, Miss Bonner," he said, "today."

Gaines went back and sat behind his desk. He swiveled his chair around so that he could look out the window at the sky. His commission from the sale of this sword was going to be considerable. So considerable, in fact, that he wasn't about to let anyone block the sale—no matter *what* he had to do.

And if that meant using Ballard, then so be it.

SIX

While Clint was getting dressed to go out that night there was a knock on his door. He had a feeling he knew who it was, and he was right. It was Karen.

"Aren't you supposed to be working?" he asked.

She pushed him back into the room, closing the door behind her as if someone were chasing her. She was dressed casually in pants and shirt that were too big for her.

"I'm supposed to start in an hour," she said, starting to unbutton her shirt.

"Hey, whoa," he said, "I'm getting dressed to go out tonight."

The young woman smiled and peeled off her shirt. She had small breasts, but they were round and firm, with dark brown nipples.

"You want me to go?" she asked.

"You little tease . . . ," he said, reaching for her.

The first time they had been together Clint had been amazed at how her breasts fit right into his hands. Given his druthers he preferred women with more meat on them, but her breasts felt so good, and *she* was so good, so energetic and inventive, that he was willing to overlook the facts that she had almost no hips, and that he could feel her ribs.

He helped her off with the rest of her clothes, and since he wasn't fully dressed yet it didn't take long for her to strip him naked, as well.

He lifted her in his arms and deposited her on the bed.

"Come here . . . ," she said, reaching for him. He came closer and she took his rigid penis first in one hand, then in both, and drew him to her. He mounted the bed and kissed her. Her mouth opened and her tongue slithered into his mouth. She slid one hand beneath his testicle sack and caressed it gently, moaning as his hands once again found her breasts and squeezed them. He rolled her nipples between his thumb and forefinger, then ran one hand down over her flat belly, through the tangle of wiry pubic hair, until he was able to slide one finger into her. With his thumb he found her clit and she jumped as if struck by lightning.

"Oh, yes . . . ," she said, opening her legs wide. He moved himself up between her slender thighs and entered her, sliding in slowly, inch by inch, until he was fully inside her and her legs were wrapped around his waist. He marveled—as he had before—at how much strength she had in legs that looked so slim.

He slid his hands beneath her to cup her buttocks. Her butt was small, but her ass cheeks were round and firm, like her breasts, only here they were *more* than a handful each.

She wrapped her arms around him, holding him to her tightly, as if he might escape. He began to move inside of her.

After that, things progressed very quickly. . . .

"Why can't we ever go slow?" Karen asked later. She was lying on his bed, watching him dress.

"Aren't you going to be late?" Clint asked.

She shrugged. She lay on her side with her elbow on a pillow, one hand supporting her head. She continued to watch him.

"They'll start without me."

"You're going to get fired."

"No, I'm not," she said, confidently. "So?"

"So what?"

"So why can't we ever go slow?"

"Because of you."

"Me?"

He sat on the bed to pull on his boots.

"You go off like fireworks, Karen," he said.

The girl laughed. "I do?"

"Oh, yeah," he said, "trying to stay with you is like trying to stay on a bucking horse."

She looked startled. "I don't know if I should be flattered, or if I should take offense. I've never been compared before to fireworks *and* a horse."

Clint leaned over and kissed her, then moved away and escaped before she could grab him.

"Be flattered," he said. "You're wonderful, it's just that you're . . . frenetic."

"What?" she asked. "What does that mean?"

"I don't know," he answered. "I heard it last week somewhere, but it sounds like it fits you."

Karen sat up, cross-legged on the bed. He stood by the door and looked at her firm breasts. The brown nipples had softened now, but when they were tight they changed drastically, getting longer. . . . And if he kept thinking about that he'd *never* get out of the room.

"I have to go," he said.

"Sure you want to leave?" she asked. One hand strayed to her right breast and she stroked it absently.

"You're a bad girl, Karen," he said.

"See you tonight?" she asked as he opened the door. She got on all fours on the bed and leaned forward, her breasts dangling slightly.

"Maybe . . . ," Clint said. His groin was already tightening again, in anticipation.

As he closed the door he heard her laughing.

SEVEN

Toshiro Matsu took some time to rest in his room after his long journey. Truly he did not feel in need of the rest, but he knew that it would do his body good. He did not sleep, but simply lay back on the bed for two hours, allowing his body to relax. His eyes never closed. He stared at the ceiling, unseeing, going over everything that had happened, and everything that *would* happen— that is, if everything happened as it *should*.

The Emperor's Sword, that's what it was all about. A *katana* with a jewel-encrusted handle, the sword was worth a fortune to anyone who wasn't Japanese. To the Japanese people it was the symbol of the Emperor's power, and none but the most foul of traitors would have stolen it and taken it to the United States to sell for *money*.

In Japan Toshiro Matsu was an enforcer of the law. Here, in this strange country, he had no more authority than a bounty hunter. He had known that, and yet he had agreed to come to this country to find the traitors and reclaim the sword. Unspoken in the Emperor's instructions was that he was also to kill the traitors—not just kill them, but *execute* them.

Matsu rose from the bed and dressed himself. He was a tall man for a Japanese, and powerfully built. He was in his forties, with a wide face and deep set eyes. His was a face without any hint of humor, for Toshiro Matsu never smiled.

He knew his clothes would be considered outlandish by the people of this country, but he felt that dressing like an American would draw even more attention to himself. Also, he *wanted* the traitors to know that he was after them. He wanted them to go in fear of him, not knowing when or where he would appear to take the Emperor's vengeance against them.

For, truly, that was what Toshiro Matsu was here to do. Although he was a lawman in his own country, he was here not only to exact justice, but to carry out a swift and deadly vengeance as well.

As for justice, his intention was to punish each man first by lopping off his hands. After that would come vengeance, when he would separate their heads from their bodies. The punishment, he felt, more than fit the seriousness of the crime.

He adjusted his *katana* on his back, checked his other weapons and left his hotel room.

EIGHT

Clint made the rounds of some of Portsmouth Square's classier gambling establishments, and in every one he saw an example of what Peter Styles had been talking about. The conversation with Styles seemed to have made him extraobservant of the foibles of the rich and very rich. Everywhere he looked he saw people who thought they were entitled to special treatment because of who they were, or how much money they had, or how much money they were losing.

After a few hours, Clint decided he needed a breath of fresh air—and the place to get it was on the Barbary Coast.

To Toshiro Matsu the Barbary Coast was a strange place. For one thing, there were women on the streets trying to sell themselves. In Japan they had prostitutes, but they did not chase men down the street, exposing their breasts and lowering their prices minute by minute.

Matsu chose to wander the Barbary Coast for two reasons: because he wanted to be seen, and also because the traitors who stole the sword would fit in with the rabble who frequented the Barbary Coast establishments.

In one place Matsu had a drink—they did *not* have rice wine—and was told by the bartender that not many "Chinee" came down to the Coast. He told Matsu that if he was looking for "friends" or "women" Chinatown would be his best bet. Matsu did not bother trying to explain to the man that he was not Chinese. All in all, for all the places he stopped in— and was stared at in—this bartender was the most helpful. It might not be a bad idea to let himself be seen in Chinatown, as well. He wondered idly if this city had a *Japan*town? Probably not.

There were still some hours to go before midnight. Matsu decided that if he did go to Chinatown, it would be on another night. Tonight he would finish his investigation of the Barbary Coast.

Clint had spent a lot of time in the past on the Barbary Coast. The pleasures the saloons along the Coast offered were simple. Women, liquor, and poker. For the most part the women were of the type he would not touch, and the whiskey the type he wouldn't drink. The poker players varied—some very bad, and some very good. If he drank, he usually drank beer.

Clint chose not to patronize one place in particular but to walk around, dropping in and out of different saloons, having a beer, watching a poker game. Of course, when you watched a poker game in a Barbary Coast saloon, you didn't watch *too* closely. Somebody was always ready to take offense.

The refreshing thing about the Barbary Coast was that, unlike the places Clint had visited earlier that evening, nobody here expected special treatment. Nobody down here thought they were better than anybody else. Fights never broke out because somebody didn't like the way somebody else was dressed, or because one person was being treated better than another. The fights down here were usually over a woman, an over-long look, or a card that may not have come out of the right deck.

When Clint entered The Deadman's Drink, he knew he was in for an unusual night. It was pretty much the same as the other saloons he had been in: dirty, bare wood floors, some tables that had seen better days, a poker game or two going on, a couple of women working the floor, a piano being badly played. Here, though, there was one significant difference.

Standing at the bar was an unusual looking man. He was Japanese, Clint knew that, and he wore the flowing garb of his country rather than Western wear. There was a full beer mug in front of the man, though he had yet to touch it.

Clint moved to the bar and settled down at the opposite end. The bartender flicked a look his way and Clint mouthed "Beer." The bartender nodded, drew him one and set it down in front of him. Clint picked up his beer and studied the

Japanese man briefly. He did not want to stare too long.

There were three men sitting at a corner table who didn't seem to feel the same way about staring. All three of them were studying the man with interest. They looked as if they were either trying to figure out where he was from or how much money he might have. The two women working the floor were also very interested in the man.

The man was not trying to speak to anyone, nor was he looking at anyone. He was simply standing at the bar, staring straight ahead. He did not seem very interested in the beer that was in front of him. Clint had the distinct feeling that, for one reason or another, the man was simply allowing himself to be seen.

Clint turned his attention once again to the three men in the corner. He saw one of them exchange a glance with two other men seated at another table across the floor. Five men, then, all with an interest in the rather still form of the Japanese gentleman.

Clint put his beer down and waited.

After about five minutes the two men seated across the floor got up and moved to the bar. They flanked the Japanese man, one on each side. Clint shifted his feet and dropped his hands down to his sides. He watched the three other men who were still seated. The two flanking the Japanese were going to have to be his own responsibility.

"Hey, bartender," one of the men said, "this fella don't seem to like your beer."

"He paid for it," the bartender said, unconcerned. "It's up to him if he wants to drink it or not."

"Yeah, well," the second man said, "as a guest in this country he shouldn't oughtta ignore our, ya know, customs."

"What customs?" the bartender asked.

"Drinkin' beer, of course," the man answered.

The bartender frowned and said, "Why don't you fellas just—"

"Hey," the first man said, pointing a finger at the bartender, "mind yer business."

The bartender shut up, picked up a dirty glass and started rubbing it with an even dirtier rag. He looked at Clint briefly and gave a small shrug.

The first man then turned to the Japanese man. "Hey, whatsamatta friend, American beer ain't good enough for ya?"

Without looking at the man the Japanese said in a deep, gruff voice, "I am not your friend." He spoke very precisely, and Clint was able to understand every word.

"Oh, izzat so?" the man said. He looked at his companion from behind the Japanese man and said, "Did you hear that, Bert? He ain't our friend."

"I heard," Bert said.

"I don't think that's very friendly, do you?"

"No, Sam, I don't."

"There's another custom you should know about in this country, pal," Sam said to the Japanese man. "You wanna know what that is?"

The Japanese did not answer.

"I'll tell you, anyway," Sam said. "When you ain't friendly you gotta pay a fine."

"Right," Bert said, "a fine."

Now the Japanese asked, "How much of a fine?"

"Well," Sam said, exchanging an amused glance with his friend Bert, "How about whatever you got on you?"

"I will pay no fine," the Japanese said.

"Yeah," Sam said, "I think you will . . . *friend.*"

Sam lifted his arm for a backhand blow to the neck of the Japanese, but faster than Clint's eye could follow the Japanese man's right hand came up and caught Sam's wrist.

"Hey!" Sam said. He tried to move his arm, but the Japanese was holding it completely immobile. Clint watched the Japanese man's face. When a small frown appeared on it he knew the man was exerting pressure.

"H-hey," Sam said, "ow, gawdamn, he's breakin' my wrist!"

The three seated men stood up, two so fast that their chairs fell over backwards.

That's when Clint drew his gun.

NINE

"Just stand easy, boys," Clint said.

"This ain't none of your affair," one of the three men said.

"I'm making it my affair," Clint said. "Five against one just doesn't strike me as very fair odds."

"You are interfering," the Japanese man said to Clint.

"I beg your pardon?" Clint said.

"Do not interfere."

Clint frowned.

"Jesus," Sam said during the silence.

"You heard the man," one of the three said. "Butt out of it."

"Okay," Clint said, reluctantly, but as the three men went for their guns he added, "but no guns."

"What?" the spokesman for the three demanded.

"I said, no guns," Clint said. "Toss 'em."

The three men stared at Clint, and then the spokesman said, "Get rid of 'em, boys. We won't need 'em, anyway."

The three men drew their guns and tossed them away.

"You, too," Clint said to Bert. He, too, took out his gun and flung it away from him.

Clint took a few steps and relieved Sam of his gun as well.

"Okay," he said, stepping back and holstering his weapon, "go ahead."

The first thing Clint heard was the sound of Sam's wrist cracking.

As the three men charged from their table the Japanese turned and swept Bert's legs out from under him. Bert went down, slamming his chin on the top of the bar. Whether that was planned or not, it knocked him out cold, and suddenly it was three against one instead of the original five.

Clint relaxed a bit and watched with interest.

The three men continued their charge, and instead of ducking or sidestepping, the Japanese moved to meet them. Clint was amazed as the first man seemed to fly over the bar, even though it seemed the Japanese had hardly touched him. It was as if the man's own momentum had carried him up and forward.

The Japanese grabbed one of the other men by the throat in a viselike grip. The third man fell prey to a well-timed kick that caught him in the pit of the stomach, driving all the air out of his lungs.

The man who had landed behind the bar climbed up on top of the bar and leaped. He had intended to jump onto the back of the Japanese man, but suddenly his quarry was not there. He came down flat on a table top, and the table collapsed beneath him.

Now there were only the Japanese and the man he was holding by the throat.

"Hey," the captive man said, "c'mon—"

Apparently, the hold was not tight enough to cut off his air, but he still could not get away. He had hold of the Japanese man's arm with both of his hands, but could not dislodge it.

"What were your intentions?" the Japanese man asked.

"Wha—"

"Were you going to rob me?"

"Yeah, yeah," the man said, "we wuz gonna rob you."

"And you would have killed me," the Japanese said, "if this other man had not interfered?"

"What? Kill you? Naw, we wasn't going to kill you," the man lied.

"I should snap your neck," the Japanese said, shaking the man.

"H-hey, c'mon, friend," the captive man said, "we wuz just, ya know, tryin' to make a livin'."

"You make your living stealing from others?"

"Well, uh, yeah, sometimes—"

Suddenly, the Japanese man's arm shot out and his captive went flying away from him. Backpedalling furiously, he was not able to keep his balance or slow his momentum and was slammed against the wall. He bounced off the wall once, then fell to the floor, stunned.

"Bah!" the Japanese said. "You are not worthy of my attention."

"Game's over, boys," Clint said. "Pick yourselves up and get out."

The few other patrons in the bar who had watched the incident now moved back to their tables, eyeing the Japanese man warily.

As the five men picked themselves up—some with the assistance of others—and slunk out of the saloon, Clint moved over next to the Japanese man.

"That was very impressive."

The Japanese looked at him. "You should not have interfered."

"Well," Clint said, trying to sound reasonable, "I was only trying to help. After all, they had guns and all you had was this interesting looking sword."

"I would have been fine."

"Against their guns?" Clint asked. "How would you have defended yourself against—"

Suddenly the Japanese whirled around and something shot across the room. It hit the wall, imbedding itself there. A few men ducked, some others just stared. Clint, interested, walked over to the wall to see what it was.

Sticking out of the wall was a star-shaped piece of metal, still quivering slightly. When Clint touched it, he cut his middle finger on its edge. Being more careful this time, he gripped it and pulled it free, carrying it back to the Japanese. It was like a star-shaped throwing knife.

"Here," Clint said, handing it back. "What is that called?"

"*Shuriken*," the Japanese replied.

"Shur-ee-kin?" Clint repeated.

"Yes," the man said. "You would call it—" he paused a moment, cocked his head, and then said, "—a throwing star."

"How many of those do you have?"

The Japanese man tucked it away somewhere within the folds of his robe. "Enough," he said.

Clint shrugged. "Well, I guess I *shouldn't* have interfered."

The Japanese hesitated a few seconds before he spoke. "No, I apologize. You were simply trying to help. I should not have spoken so harshly."

"That's okay," Clint said. "Look, why don't you let me buy you a fresh beer? We can sit down and talk a bit. I'm very interested in you—uh, well, in what you're doing here in this country. Who knows? Maybe I can even help you."

The Japanese thought about it a moment, then nodded and said gruffly, "*Hai.*"

Clint assumed that meant yes and ordered two fresh beers.

TEN

The two men walked to the corner table recently vacated by three of the attackers. Clint righted a couple of chairs and they sat down with their beers.

"How long have you been in this country?" Clint asked.

"I arrived today," Matsu said.

"My name is Clint Adams," Clint introduced himself, extending his hand.

The Japanese accepted the hand, shook it briefly but firmly and said, "I am Toshiro Matsu."

"It's a pleasure to meet you," Clint said. "What brings you to this country . . ." Clint wasn't sure what to call the man—Mr. Matsu? Mr. Toshiro?—so he just let the question trail off.

"I am hunting," Matsu said.

"For what?"

"Criminals," Matsu answered. "Traitors."

"Countrymen of yours, I assume," Clint said.

"Yes."

"This is interesting. Are you a lawman of some sort?"

"In my country, yes," Matsu said. "Here, in your country, I have no authority."

"No, I don't suppose you would," Clint responded. "Uh, can you tell me what these men did?"

Matsu seemed to consider the question for a few moments. He then nodded to himself, as if he had come to a decision.

"I will tell you," he said, "but first I would ask you a question."

"Sure," Clint said, "go ahead."

"Why did you help me?"

Clint sat back. "Because you were outnumbered. I thought you *needed* help."

"And what did you expect in return?"

"Nothing," Clint said. "Maybe a 'thank you,' but nothing beyond that. Why does someone need to get something in return for helping someone who's in trouble?"

"I did not expect to find such attitudes here," the Japanese man replied.

"Well, I don't know how common it is, but it's *my* attitude."

"I will answer your question now," said Matsu.

The Japanese lawman told Clint about the theft of the Emperor's Sword, and how he had tracked the thieves to a ship that had already left Japan and was heading for the United States. Matsu had caught the very next ship and come here after them.

"And you only got here today," Clint said.

"Yes."

"Do you have any leads?"

Matsu frowned. "Leads?"

"Uh, have you found a trail to follow?"

"No, I have not," Matsu said. "I suspect that the man who works in my hotel may know something. Also, a bartender advised me to look in Chinatown."

"Sounds like good advice," Clint said. "Even though the men you seek are Japanese, that would be the best place in this city to hide out. Uh, of course they wouldn't be able to stay dressed like you are."

"They would wear Western clothes."

"Yes."

Matsu looked down at himself.

"I suspect," Clint said, "that what you were doing was letting yourself be seen, so that it would get back to them. You *want* them to know you're after them, right?"

Matsu nodded. "That is what I was thinking, yes."

"Well, it's not a bad plan," Clint said.

Matsu waited, then asked, "But?"

"Well, it just seems to me you're making too much of a target of yourself."

"For them?"

"For them," Clint said, "for thieves like the ones you just dealt with—and you don't need the extra attention, believe me. Do you have American money?"

"Yes," Matsu said, "some."

"Well, if I was you I'd buy some Western clothes and *then* go looking in Chinatown."

Matsu thought about that a moment, then nodded. "I will buy some clothes. Can you tell me a place where I may do so?" he asked.

"Sure," Clint answered. "I can take you there and help you pick something out, if you like."

"Yes," Matsu said, "I am a stranger here. I will accept any assistance you would be willing to give me."

"I'll help you all I can, uh, Matsu? Can I call you that?"

"Yes," Matsu said, "that is fine."

"Okay, you can call me Clint. Would you like to go and buy those clothes now?"

"Yes, please," Matsu replied. "And I would like you to talk about yourself."

"Myself?" Clint asked as they stood up.

"Yes," Matsu said. "If you are going to help me, or are offering your friendship, we should talk about ourselves, should we not?"

"I suppose that's true, Matsu," Clint said. "Yeah, okay, come on, we'll talk on the way."

ELEVEN

Clint took Matsu to a men's clothing store. They bought him some inexpensive clothes, which he put on in the store. They then rolled his Japanese clothes into a ball and went back to Matsu's hotel to drop them off.

"You're staying here?" Clint asked, looking over the room.

"Yes," Matsu replied. "Is it not appropriate?"

"Well," Clint said, "you're a stranger in town, Matsu—I mean, you're *really* a stranger in town— and while I know you can take care of yourself, you don't need the extra added, uh, pressure of having to watch your back."

"Watch my back?"

"Down around here they have a special way of treating strangers," Clint said, "like those fellas in the saloon, you know what I mean?"

"There are a lot of thieves?"

"Yes," Clint said, "a *lot* of thieves."

"Then you think I should stay somewhere else?" Matsu asked.

"I would suggest it, yes."

"And where would you suggest I stay?"

Clint smiled at Matsu. "I have just the place. Get your things."

Clint took Toshiro Matsu back to The Clapton House and got him a room. The desk clerk gave them both a strange look—especially Matsu who, though dressed now in Western garb, still looked very much Japanese. His hair was long, and they had not bought him a hat, and he still wore his *katana* slung across his back.

"Is Mr. Styles around?" Clint asked the clerk.

"I believe he's away from the hotel right now, Mr. Adams," the clerk said.

"All right," Clint said, "we can talk to him in the morning."

"Yes, sir," the man said. "Is there anything you would like me to tell him?"

"No, thank you," Clint said. "I'll take care of it myself in the morning. I'll just show Mr. Matsu to his room."

Clint took Matsu up to the second floor, where his own room was. In fact, the Japanese man's room was just down the hall from his.

Once inside the room Matsu looked around. He said, "This is much nicer."

"Yes, it is," Clint agreed, "and it's in a better neighborhood."

"No thieves?"

Clint hesitated. "Well, no, I wouldn't say that. There are still thieves, but they're not as . . . aggressive."

"Who is Mr. Styles?" Matsu asked.

"He manages this hotel," Clint said, "and he's a friend of mine. I want to talk to him about you."

"Why?"

"Well, he might want to help you, too."

"Why?"

"Because you're a stranger, and you need help . . . and he's a helpful man."

"Like you."

"Yes," Clint said, "like me. Why don't we turn in now and we can see Styles in the morning, at breakfast."

"What about Chinatown?" Matsu asked.

"We can go to Chinatown tomorrow," Clint said, "when it's light."

"We?" Matsu asked. "You will be going with me?"

"Well . . . I thought I might. I sort of feel like you're a guest in my country, and I should show you around some. That is, if you don't mind."

"I don't mind," Matsu said. "I welcome your assistance."

"Good," Clint said. "Let's get some sleep, then."

"I thank you for the help you have given me this night," Matsu said, with a slight bow.

Clint didn't know how to react, so he simply said, "I was glad to help, Matsu. Good night."

"Good night."

When Clint Adams had left the room, Toshiro Matsu reached down to test the mattress on the bed. It more than met with his approval, especially considering the mattress that had been in his other room. However, he rarely slept on a mattress in his own country. He looked down at the floor, then back at the bed. Finally he decided that it would be rude to Clint Adams, his host, for him to disdain it now.

Clint left Matsu's room and walked down the hall to his own. He was somewhat amazed at how easily he had ended up being Toshiro Matsu's host here in the United States. He just hadn't liked seeing the man set upon by five men, especially on the very day he had arrived.

In his own room he thought about the jewel encrusted Emperor's Sword that Matsu was here searching for. Also the thieves—or traitors, as Matsu put it—who had stolen it. Clint had a feeling that Matsu was very good with that sword he wore on his back. He was glad that *he* wasn't one of the men Toshiro Matsu was hunting.

TWELVE

Clint had been in his room for half an hour when there was a knock on his door. It was a familiar knock, a woman's knock. It was the way Karen knocked every time she came to his room after work.

Even though he recognized the knock, he took his gun with him to the door, the holster slung over his shoulder casually. That way it was there if he needed it, but didn't necessarily look menacing.

She smiled as he opened the door. "Still afraid of me, huh?"

He stepped back to let her in. He had explained to her a few times that he had to be careful, but he allowed her her little joke.

She closed the door and turned to face him.

"Boy," she said, "I'm beat."

"Go to bed," he said.

"That's what I had in mind."

"I meant," he said, "to sleep."

"So did I," she said, then added, "eventually, that is."

She had already abandoned her work clothes, the low-cut dress she always wore. She was once again wearing the shirt and trousers that were too large for her. Now she unbuttoned her shirt and allowed it to fall to the floor. As always, her naked breasts had the desired effect on Clint, who was no longer thinking about the bed as a place to sleep.

Clint moved to her and palmed her breasts. Immediately, he felt the nipples harden. Karen let her head fall back and moaned. He was amazed at how sensitive her breasts and nipples were. More often than not she experienced a small ripple of pleasure while he was mouthing her breasts, biting and sucking her nipples. He had run into that with other women, but not so often, and it amazed and delighted him.

He pulled her shoes off, then her trousers and underwear. When she was naked he encircled her with his arms and picked her up, carrying her to the bed while working on her chocolate-tipped breasts with his mouth.

He set her down on the bed. She said, "Hurry, hurry . . ." as he started to take off his own clothes. Her hands ran up her slender body to cup her own breasts, flicking the nipples with her thumbs. Clint wondered how far she would go if he *didn't* join her on the bed, but she wasn't about to allow that. She reached out, took hold of him, and when she tugged he had no choice but to go where she wanted him to go. . . .

• • •

"I made a new friend," Clint said, later.

Karen pinched the flesh on his side and said, "Another woman?"

"No," he answered, "not another woman. A man. A Japanese man."

"Japanese?"

"He just got off the boat today from Japan," Clint said.

"What's he doin' here?" she asked, snuggling against him, sleepily.

"Hunting."

"For what?"

"A sword," Clint said, "and some men who stole it."

"A sword?" she asked. "Why would anyone steal a sword?"

"Apparently," he said, "in Japan this is an extremely important sword. It's the symbol of the Emperor's power, or something."

"An emperor? He doesn't have any power without some sword? He doesn't sound like much of an emperor to me."

Clint was thinking the same thing, but he was willing to concede that maybe he and Karen just didn't understand the Japanese culture. He certainly wasn't about to tell Toshiro Matsu that he didn't think much of his Emperor. After all, the man had come all this way at his Emperor's request, and Toshiro Matsu struck Clint as the very loyal type.

THIRTEEN

Daryl Gaines looked down at the top of Althea Bonner's head between his bare legs. They were both naked in bed at the Palace Hotel, where he kept a room for just this purpose.

By the end of his business day, Gaines was annoyed. Ballard had not appeared. He had asked Miss Bonner twice more to send for him, which she did, and still he had not appeared.

Gaines understood men like Ballard. They worked for money, but they did not want to seem to *need* the money. This was Ballard's way of telling Gaines that he did not need his money. Ordinarily Gaines didn't mind playing the man's games, but he felt now that the situation called for quick action, not games.

So annoyed had Gaines been that he had sent word home to his wife that he would be working late. He took Althea Bonner to the hotel with him. First he had stripped her forcefully, pushed her down onto all fours and taken her from behind. He had been brutal, taking out his frustrations on her. But Althea Bonner knew who paid her salary, and she not only endured it but—he was sure—enjoyed it.

Now she was eagerly working on his rigid penis, her head rising and falling with increased speed while he held it between his hands.

While working on her boss Althea Bonner chose to think about her boyfriend. She was able to close her eyes without his knowing, just as she had been able to do while on all fours before him. While he rutted from behind her she had tried to imagine that he was her boyfriend, but Daryl Gaines was incapable of giving her the same pleasure that her boyfriend gave her. To Gaines she was just a receptacle, while to her boyfriend she was the woman he loved. Althea endured the attentions of her boss because of the lavish salary he paid her. She hoped to save enough money so that she and her boyfriend could get married. She knew, however, that if her boyfriend ever found out about this he'd probably *kill* Daryl Gaines. She didn't want that. That would be like killing the goose that laid the golden eggs.

So she made excuses to her boyfriend about working late on the nights that Gaines took her to the Palace Hotel, just as Gaines lied to his wife.

Gaines tightened his hold on Althea Bonner's head, then pushed down as he exploded into her mouth. At that moment there was a knock on the door. He opened his eyes wide. For one second he wondered if it were his wife, but that was impossible.

"Get off," he said, pushing Althea off to the side.

He swung his legs to the floor and grabbed his dressing gown. He couldn't see Althea Bonner as she hung her head over the side of the bed and spit his seed onto the floor, wiping her mouth with the back of her hand.

Gaines donned the dressing gown and walked to the door. He opened the door slowly, just a crack, in case it *was* his wife, Mary. He was already thinking up a plausible lie to tell her when he saw that it was not Mary, but Wade Ballard, who was standing in the hall.

"You wanted to see me?" Ballard asked.

"Jesus . . . ," Gaines said.

"I catch you at a bad time?" Ballard asked.

"Wait for me downstairs, Wade," Gaines said. "I'll only be a couple of minutes."

Ballard frowned but said, "I'll wait in the bar."

Gaines closed the door and turned to look at Althea Bonner, who was now sitting cross-legged on the bed, watching him. "Get dressed!" he barked.

FOURTEEN

The next morning Clint slid free of Karen's arms and legs, which she had wrapped around him in her sleep. He managed to disentangle himself without waking her, then washed himself thoroughly using the basin and pitcher of water that always seemed to be full when he needed it. That was the mark of a good hotel.

He got dressed and started down the hall to Toshiro Matsu's room. Just as he reached the door it opened. The Japanese man filled the doorway.

"Oh," Clint said, "I was just coming to see if you were awake."

"I know," Matsu said. "I heard you. I have been awake for a long time."

"Did you sleep at all?"

"Yes," Matsu said, "but I require only a few hours of sleep."

"That probably comes in handy," Clint said, "in your business."

Toshiro Matsu turned his back to Clint as he closed the door. Clint saw the sword on his back and admired it.

"Tell me," Clint asked, "do you usually eat breakfast in the morning?"

"Not usually," Matsu responded, "but I am your guest. I will force myself."

Clint regarded the man for a moment, wondering if he had suddenly detected a sense of humor. There was no hint of any such thing on Matsu's face, and for a moment Clint thought he might have imagined it. Yet when he played the words over in his mind he felt sure that they were meant as a joke. Perhaps Matsu just had a deadpan way of delivering a funny line.

"Why don't we go down to the dining room, then?" he suggested.

"What about your . . . friend?"

"My friend?"

"The woman."

"What woman?"

Matsu gave Clint a look, and while his facial expression changed very little, Clint felt that the look was one of impatience.

"The woman you shared your bed with last night," Matsu said.

"Oh, that woman," Clint said, frowning. "No, she never eats breakfast. She usually sleeps late."

"Ah . . ."

They left the room. When they reached the stairway Clint couldn't hold it back anymore.

"How did you know I had a woman with me last night? Did you see her?"

"No."

"Did we . . . make noise?"

"No."

"Well, then—"

"I smelled her."

"You smelled her?" Clint asked, looking at the man in surprise. "From down the hall?"

"No," Matsu said, "on you."

"On me?"

Clint couldn't help it. He lowered his head a bit and took a sniff. He felt he had washed himself fairly well, in the absence of a bath, and yet the Japanese insisted he could smell Karen on him.

Again, he searched the man's face for any sign that he was joking. This time, Clint felt sure that he was not joking.

"You must have a very keen sense of smell," he said to his Japanese guest.

"Yes," Matsu answered simply, "I do. It also comes in very handy in my business."

"Yes," Clint said, "I can see that it would."

FIFTEEN

Daryl Gaines stared across the breakfast table at his wife and wondered where the woman he had married had gone. The woman sitting across from him was barren. She had been able to bear him no children, and soon after she realized this she would no longer tolerate his touch. They had been married for fifteen years, now, and he was quite sure that ten of them had been loveless.

He suddenly found himself thinking of a naked Althea Bonner, when Mary Gaines asked, "What are you thinking?"

For a moment he wondered if she was able to read his mind but then came to his senses.

"Just business, Mary," he said. "Nothing for you to worry about."

She nodded and went back to her breakfast.

How could she think that everything was all right between them, he wondered? She always acted like they had a perfect marriage—and to anyone looking in from outside it probably appeared that they did. Of course, if they really wanted to know, all they'd have to do was ask *him. He'd* tell them. . . .

"Daddy asked me about you yesterday," Mary said.

God, he thought, she's over thirty and she still calls her father "Daddy."

Daddy, of course, was Walter Carpenter, one of the five richest men in San Francisco. He also had a lot of political influence, of which Daryl Gaines was determined to take advantage. After all, he deserved *something* for taking the man's daughter off his hands fifteen years ago, didn't he?

"How is he?" Gaines asked. How is the old coot, he added to himself.

"He's fine," she said. "He's coming to dinner tomorrow night."

"That's good," Gaines said.

Gaines was determined to make his way in the world. That was why he had the sideline of buying and selling valuable objects, like the Japanese sword, to men who could afford them. Little by little he was building himself a small fortune, one that he kept hidden from Mary and her Daddy. Of course, that didn't mean he *wouldn't* use Walter Carpenter's influence to get himself into politics. It only meant that after he was firmly in place—in the political sense—he would no longer need Mary or her father.

He couldn't wait for that day to come.

"Time to go to work," Gaines said, standing up.

"Kiss, kiss," Mary said.

He leaned over, closed his eyes and kissed her dry mouth quickly.

"See you later, dear," she said as he went out the door.

On his way to his office he thought of the conversation he'd had with Wade Ballard last night, after getting Althea Bonner dressed and on her way.

"Sorry to disturb you," Ballard said as he sat down beside Gaines in the saloon. Ballard had gotten himself a beer, but had ordered nothing for Gaines. Another way to thumb his nose at me, Gaines thought.

"Forget it," Gaines said, tight-lipped.

"I heard you were lookin' for me."

Gaines regarded Ballard across the table. Wade Ballard was thirty-five—Gaines's age—and had been killing men for money for sixteen years. He was good at it, and what was particularly important to a man like Gaines—who employed men like Ballard—was that Ballard *didn't* have a reputation. The man went about his business while keeping a low profile.

"It was nice of you to decide to come and see me," Gaines said, and then added, "finally."

Ballard stared at Gaines for a long moment, then smiled.

"Come on, Daryl," Ballard said. "It's all part of the game."

A game the two men had been playing for almost thirty years. Daryl remembered the first time he had hired Ballard to hurt another person. They were both eight years old, and because Ballard was big for his age he was able to break the arm of a ten-year-old boy who was picking on Gaines. Since that time Gaines had been using Ballard as a weapon, pointing him and paying him. They were both nineteen the first time Gaines hired Ballard to kill another man. Since that time Ballard had gotten so good at killing that he did it for other men as well—other men who paid him, that is.

"All right," Gaines said, "playtime is over, all right?"

"Sure, Daryl," Ballard said. "What's the job this time?"

"You ever hear of a man called Clint Adams?" Gaines asked, watching Ballard closely.

Ballard stared back at him. He said, slowly, "That's the Gunsmith."

"That's right," Gaines said, "the Gunsmith. And he's in my way, Wade."

Ballard looked away from Gaines, but not *at* anything in particular. He was looking inward, at something only he could see.

Ballard was thinking. It had never been his desire to make a spectacle of himself; he had never wanted credit for the men he killed. It was enough for him that he got paid for killing, and that he enjoyed doing it. Each time it was a new challenge to him. And this—killing the Gunsmith—was the ultimate challenge.

"Think about it, man," Gaines said, watching Wade Ballard closely. "If you were a man who was after a reputation, Wade—"

"But I'm not," Ballard said, cutting him off. "We both know that."

"No," Gaines said, "you'd appreciate this just

for the challenge, wouldn't you?"

"And the money," Ballard said.

"Oh, yes, there's the money," Gaines said.

"How much money are we talking about here, Daryl?" Ballard asked.

"Oh, I think enough, Wade," Gaines said, "I think enough."

Of course, Gaines thought now as he mounted the stairs to his office, it hadn't been enough, but they had been able to work that out. When Ballard got the job done, it would be money well spent.

SIXTEEN

When Clint and Matsu reached the dining room Peter Styles was already seated at his table with a pot of coffee. He had not yet, however, begun to eat his breakfast.

Even clad in Western clothes, Toshiro Matsu commanded attention. For one thing he was Japanese, and for another he was a *big* Japanese.

Styles, as if he sensed that something unusual was happening in the room, looked up from his newspaper and frowned when he saw Clint and Matsu approaching his table. It was not a displeased frown, but a puzzled one. It was the kind of look where, if looks could speak, this one would say, "What the hell—"

"Peter Styles," Clint said, "my new friend from Japan, Toshiro Matsu."

"Mr. Matsu," Styles said. He stood and extended his hand. Matsu hesitated just a split second, then took it and shook it firmly. "Welcome to our country," the hotel manager continued. He indicated the other chairs at the table. "Please, sit. Join me for breakfast."

"Thank you," Matsu said.

As they all sat down Felix came over with extra cups and saucers and another pot of coffee.

"I'm sorry," Styles said to Matsu. "Would you prefer something else? Tea, maybe?"

"I have tasted your American coffee before," Matsu replied. "It will be fine."

"Good," Styles said, and Felix poured out three cups.

"What can we get you gentlemen for breakfast?" Styles asked Clint and Matsu.

"I'll have the usual, Felix," Clint told the waiter. He turned and explained to Matsu what his "usual" was.

"That will be fine," Matsu said.

Styles sipped his coffee, regarding his guests over the rim of the cup.

"Matsu is a guest in the hotel now, Peter," Clint said. "I brought him here from a Barbary Coast hotel."

"I hope you like it better here," Styles said to Toshiro Matsu.

"I am sure I will."

"What brings you to our country, Mr. Matsu?" Styles asked him.

"I am hunting for two men," Matsu said.

"Countrymen of yours?"

"Yes," the Japanese answered. "Traitors, and thieves."

"I see."

"I've offered him my help," Clint told Styles, "since he doesn't know the city at all."

"Clint knows San Francisco fairly well," Styles

said to Matsu. "He's been here often enough."

"I am grateful for his help," Matsu said.

"We had an interesting experience last night," Clint said, and explained about Matsu facing the five men in the saloon.

"It does sound interesting," said Styles. He looked at Matsu. "You sound very capable, sir."

Matsu executed a seated bow, accepting the compliment gracefully.

Breakfast was served and the three men ate. Styles was still curious. He felt sure that there was a request in the offing, or else why would Clint have brought the Japanese down for breakfast?

"Tell me," he said, when they were almost finished with breakfast, "is there anything I can do to help?"

Clint and Matsu exchanged glances. Clint said, "I'll be taking Matsu to Chinatown today. Although he and his countrymen are *Japan*ese, Chinatown might be the place they'd seek shelter."

"That's a good point," Styles said. "They might stand out to the Chinese, but to most white men—I'm sorry to say—all Orientals look alike."

"I can appreciate that," Matsu replied. "There is no need to apologize."

"Do you know anyone in Chinatown who might help?" Clint asked.

"Don't you know a couple of Chinese detectives in Chinatown?" Styles asked in turn.

"I checked when I got here, Peter, and they're both out of town," Clint said.

"Well . . . I *might* know someone, but whether or not he will help you is . . . debatable."

"We can ask," Clint said. "All he can do is say no. What's his name?"

"His name is Nok Woo Lee," Styles told him. "Or you can just call him Lee. You'll find him in Ross Alley." He gave them an address.

"What does he do?" Clint asked.

"Everything and anything," Styles answered, "for money. You'll doubtless have to pay him."

"I have money," Matsu said. "That will not be a problem."

"All right," Styles said. "After breakfast I'll write you a letter of introduction. Without it, he might not see you."

"We appreciate it, Peter."

Styles spread his arms apart slightly. "I'm just trying to be a good host, Clint."

"And that you are, Peter," Clint said, raising his coffee cup. "I've always said that."

SEVENTEEN

Armed with Peter Styles's letter of introduction, Clint took Toshiro Matsu to Chinatown. It was there that Clint first noticed the difference between Matsu, a Japanese, and the Chinese people. Beyond the fact that their eyes were shaped differently, most of the Chinese looked gentle, even meek, while Matsu looked anything but meek.

"Can I ask you a question?" Clint asked.

"Of course," Matsu said, executing a short bow. Clint assumed that the bow was some sort of display of manners or respect.

"Are you large for your, uh, people? I mean, are most Japanese smaller than you, or are you, uh, average?"

"I am considered to be large among my people," Matsu answered. "Most of them are as you see here, smaller than you and I."

"I see."

"Do you think that I look like them?" Matsu asked, indicating the people around them.

"Well, actually, no," Clint said. "I think you

60

look very different from them. In fact, I think you and I would have an equally hard time blending in here among these people. Together, we have no chance of going unnoticed."

"I do not wish to go unnoticed," replied Matsu.

"I know that's still your strategy," Clint said. "But I think it's better if we don't stick out like a sore thumb."

Matsu looked at his thumb and then frowned at Clint.

"It was just something that came to mind," Clint said. "Never mind."

They were walking toward Ross Alley when Matsu noticed a small, elderly Chinese man stop and openly stare at him. He approached the man and took hold of his arm.

"Aieeee!" the man said, trying to pull away.

Clint turned and said, "Wha—"

"You have seen others like me?" Matsu asked the old man.

The man began to jabber in his native tongue while continuing to pull away from Matsu. Around them others stopped to stare, talking amongst themselves. Clint didn't like the idea of a crowd building.

"Matsu," he said, coming up next to the Japanese man.

"He was looking at me strangely," Matsu stated. "He has seen the others."

"Maybe he's just never seen anyone like you." Clint put his hand on Matsu's arm, the one he was using to hold the small Chinese man fast. "Let him go, Matsu."

The Japanese man looked at Clint, but did not release the old man.

"Let him go," Clint said again, firmly.

Matsu stared at Clint a little longer, then released the little man without looking at him. Still jabbering, the old man scurried away.

"You can't do that," Clint said, taking his hand off of Matsu's arm.

The Japanese seemed about to say something. But he suddenly looked away and then down.

"I apologize," he said. "You are my host and I have embarassed you—"

"Oh, cut the crap, Matsu," Clint said. "Don't act subservient to me. It doesn't fit you. I know your people are polite, but I get the feeling more often than not you'd rather just speak your mind."

Matsu continued to stare down, then turned his head and looked Clint in the eye. In that moment Clint felt a chill. He reminded himself never to get Toshiro Matsu angry at him.

"Can we go?" he asked.

"Yes," Matsu said, "we go."

Clint turned and led the way towards Ross Alley, feeling like he'd just successfully dodged a bullet—this time.

EIGHTEEN

Following the instructions given them by Peter Styles, Clint found the building they wanted on Ross Alley. From the outside it didn't look like anyone lived there. It looked more like an abandoned warehouse.

"Is this the right place?" Matsu asked, staring at the edifice strangely.

"It's supposed to be," Clint said. "Let's find out."

They turned to face the thick wooden door and Clint knocked on it. When there was no answer he knocked louder, actually pounding on it this time.

At about eye level there was a small cutout in the door. This opened abruptly, revealing a set of dark eyes looking out at them.

"Who are you?"

"My name's Clint Adams," Clint said.

"So?"

"I have a letter, here," Clint said, holding the letter up.

"Push it through," the man said, and the eyes disappeared.

Clint looked at Matsu, then slid the envelope through the opening. He heard the letter being unfolded, and assumed it was being read. Suddenly, the eyes reappeared, and they were looking at Matsu.

"Who's he?"

"A friend," Clint said. "Toshiro Matsu."

"Do you know what this letter says?" the man asked.

"No," Clint answered truthfully. Styles had written it and then slid it into the envelope without offering to let him read it first.

"What were you told?"

"Just a name," Clint said.

"What name?"

"Nok Woo Lee," Clint replied, "or just Lee."

Clint heard a lock being turned, and the thick door swung inward. When the man appeared Clint was surprised. He'd expected a Chinese, but this man was white. There wasn't even any kind of half caste to him. He was full-blooded white.

"Are you Lee?" Clint asked.

"That's right," Lee said. "Come on in—both of you."

The man backed away to allow them to enter. They found themselves in a cramped hallway. They waited for Lee to relock the door and turn to face them.

"Please," he said, "just walk ahead of me to the door at the end of the hall."

Clint turned and followed his instructions.

Matsu followed him, and Lee brought up the rear.

When they reached the door Clint opened it and they stepped into a well-lighted, high-ceilinged room that was obviously used as a living quarters.

Lee moved around them into the center of the room.

"Please," he said, "sit."

There was no furniture, but there were pillows everywhere. Clint picked one and sat on it. Matsu sat next to him, but ignored the pillows and sat directly on the floor.

Clint took a moment to examine the man standing before them. Not only wasn't he Chinese, but he was rather unremarkable looking—and younger than Clint had expected. Nok Woo Lee—if that was indeed his name—was about thirty, stood no more than five foot ten and was slender. He could have been a school teacher, if it weren't for his eyes. They were dark, and cold, and Clint got the feeling that they had seen a lot of hardship and pain. He was wearing the coolie "pajamas" a lot of the Chinese in Chinatown wore.

"If you're curious," Lee said, "ask."

"My guess," Clint said, speaking his mind, "would be that you were raised Chinese, I just don't know if it was here, or in China."

"Very good," Lee said.

"Here?" Clint asked.

"It was in China," Nok Woo Lee told him. "I was born on a ship and left behind by my real parents, who didn't want me. They gave me to a Chinese family, who raised me as their own. When I was old enough I got back on a ship and came here."

"Why?" Matsu asked.

Lee looked at Matsu. "To find the bastard and the bitch who left me behind."

"To do what?" Matsu asked.

"To kill them," Lee answered coolly.

"Did you?" Clint asked.

"Not yet."

"Are you still looking?" Clint asked.

"Yes," Lee said, looking back at Clint, "I haven't given up, even though it's been over thirty years."

"They might be dead already," Clint said.

"That occurred to me," Lee said, "but that doesn't mean I'll stop looking. In the meanwhile, I have to make a living."

"Doing what?"

Lee shrugged his shoulders and said, "Suppose you tell me? My guess is that's what you're here for."

Clint looked at Matsu. "Would you like me to tell him?"

Matsu nodded, bowing to Clint's superior knowledge of the English language, and said, "Please."

NINETEEN

Clint outlined the story briefly for Lee, who listened quietly and intently. He did not ask any questions until Clint had finished talking. He also moved very little while he listened. While speaking Clint noticed that the man was barefoot.

"That's very interesting," Lee said when Clint had finished speaking.

"Have you heard of two such men?" Matsu asked.

"I hear many things," Lee said. The way he said it made Clint suddenly realize that English was not the man's first language. "I usually hear about strangers."

"And these?" Clint asked.

Lee frowned. "I haven't heard about these, which is odd. If they are here I *should* have heard about them. That can only mean one thing."

"Somebody's hiding them," said Clint.

"Correct," Lee answered.

"Can you find them?" Matsu asked.

Lee looked from Clint to Matsu and back, and then spoke to the Japanese man.

"Is that what you want me to do?"

"Yes."

"Is that *all* you want me to do?" Lee asked.

Matsu frowned.

"I do not understand."

"I think I do," Clint said. "I think Mr. Lee—"

"Just Lee," the man said.

"All right," Clint said. "I think that Lee is sort of a full-service individual. If you want him to find them, he will. If you want him to kill them after he's found them, he'll do that too. Am I right?"

"Yes," Lee said, simply.

"And the more you do, the higher the fee."

"Naturally."

"I do not want you to kill them," Matsu said. "I will take care of them myself."

"As you wish," Lee said, executing a polite little bow, just a slight move from the waist. "Can I interest you gentlemen in some tea while we discuss my fee?"

"Sure," Clint said, wishing for something stronger. "Tea would be just fine."

"Matsu?" Lee asked.

"Yes," Matsu said, "fine."

Clint watched as Lee moved around, preparing the tea and bringing it to them. He was remarkably light on his feet. Clint imagined that he would be very deadly in a bar fight—or any kind of conflict. Although he was shorter and lighter than Matsu, Clint wondered idly what would happen if Lee and Matsu got into a fight.

Where would he put his money? Probably on the larger man, but he would like to see Lee in action before actually placing his bet.

Over tea Lee quoted some figures, depending on just how much he was required to do. Clint might have argued some, tried to bargain him down, but Matsu did not have the patience for that. He readily agreed to Lee's fee, and paid half of it on the spot.

"If you find that you have a need for me—for, uh, any of my other talents," Lee said, "you have just to let me know."

Matsu gave Lee an appraising glance. "I do not think so."

It was said in such a way that Clint sat up straight and studied Lee to see how he would react.

"What do you mean by that?" Lee asked.

"I did not mean anything," Matsu said. "These are dangerous men. I will have to deal with them myself, to be sure that, uh, they are dealt with in a, er, proper fashion."

Lee studied Matsu coldly. "Are you saying that you don't think I could handle them? That I can't handle myself?"

"I don't think he meant that at—"

"Let him answer!" Lee said, staring directly at Matsu. "Let the . . . *Japanese* answer."

The way Lee said "Japanese" made Clint lean forward and study Matsu. Clint did not know if there was some sort of traditional conflict between the Chinese and Japanese, but he was starting to get that feeling.

"I do not know your capabilities," Matsu said slowly. "I do know mine, and I can trust them."

"Would you like to test my capabilities?" Lee asked Matsu.

Matsu stared right back at Lee unwaveringly. Clint was about to try to step between them again—figuratively speaking—when Matsu said, "Perhaps another time."

Lee stared back. He said, "Sure, another time, maybe *after* our business is completed—after your business is taken care of. You can come back here anytime, Mr. Matsu, and I'll *show* you my capabilities."

Clint and Matsu stood up. Lee and Matsu actually bowed politely to each other.

"I will contact you at your hotel when I know anything," Lee said, walking them to the door.

Outside Clint asked, "What was all that about? Is there a problem between the Japanese and the Chinese?"

"There was," Matsu said, "a long time ago."

"But not now?"

"No," Matsu said, somewhat unconvincingly, "not now."

The Japanese quickened his pace and walked on ahead of Clint.

"Well, that's good," Clint said to his back. "I'd hate to think how the two of you might have acted if there was."

TWENTY

There didn't seem to be much sense in doing
anything but going back to the hotel. Matsu was
quiet all the way back, and as soon as they entered
the hotel he went up to his room without a word
to Clint.

"You're welcome," Clint said to his back as the
Japanese man climbed the stairs.

He turned and walked to the desk.

"Where's Mr. Styles?" he asked the clerk.

"In his office, sir," the man said. "Shall I tell
him you're here?"

"No, thanks," Clint said, "I'll tell him myself."

Clint moved around the desk. The clerk wasn't
quite sure what to do. He knew Clint was a guest,
but he also knew that he was a friend of the boss.
In the end he simply moved out of the way and
hoped he was doing the right thing.

Clint went through a curtained doorway behind
the desk and made his way down a hallway to
Peter Styles's office. He knocked on the door and
entered. Styles was seated behind his desk. He
looked up from his work.

"Back already?" he asked.

Clint didn't answer. He walked to the chair opposite Styles's desk and sat down. Styles signed something on his desk, then put his pen down and leaned back.

"Sherry?" he asked.

"I'd like something stronger."

"The saloon will be open in a half an hour," Styles said. "What's on your mind?"

"Your friend, Lee."

"Interesting fellow, no?"

"Sure," Clint said, "if you like hired killers."

Styles winced. "That's not the way I think of him, Clint."

"Oh? How do you think of him?"

"As a man who provides a variety of services," Styles said, as if he didn't need to think about it at all—and obviously he didn't.

"And killing is one of them."

Styles spread his hands helplessly. "I can honestly say that I've never hired him to kill anyone, and I've never heard of him hiring out to kill anyone."

"He made the offer to us, Peter!" Clint said. "I was there."

"Maybe he thought that was what you wanted."

Clint frowned and decided not to argue this point with his friend.

"He also tried to pick a fight with Matsu."

"Really?" Styles asked. He pressed his palms and fingers flat together and touched the tips of his index fingers to his lips thoughtfully. "From what you tell me about your friend Matsu, that would be an interesting contest."

"Sure," Clint said, "if your idea of fun is a fight to the death."

"Aren't you exaggerating?"

"They don't like each other, Peter," Clint said. "Apparently, the Japanese and Chinese don't particularly get along as peoples, and while Lee is not Chinese in appearance, he certainly is in every other way."

"Well, I'd certainly have to agree with that."

Clint shook his head and said, "I don't know, Peter."

"About what?"

"I have a real problem with a man who is searching for his own parents in order to kill them."

"After they deserted him at birth?" Styles asked. "I don't have a problem with that."

Clint stared at Styles, who seemed fairly adamant on that point. He wondered if Lee and Styles had something in common.

"Well . . ." Clint said, as the silence between them grew awkward.

"Well," Styles said.

"Thanks for your help."

"If it helps."

"Oh, it'll help," Clint replied, standing up. "I think if Matsu's two renegades are in San Francisco your friend Lee will find them."

"If they're still here," Styles said. "My guess is they're here—in this country—to sell that sword to the highest bidder. What if the highest bidder isn't in San Francisco?"

"Good point," Clint conceded, "but they haven't been here that long. Maybe they haven't found a buyer yet."

"You know . . ." Styles said, his words trailing off while his mind worked.

"What?"

Clint's question seemed to bring Styles back from another place.

"I was just thinking," he said, "how many dealers in stolen articles could there be in San Francisco?"

"I don't know," Clint answered, "but you sound like you think you could find out."

"Maybe," Styles said.

"I'm sure Matsu will appreciate anything you can do," said Clint. "Although," he added, "he seems to have a funny way of showing appreciation."

Styles looked at his watch and then stood up.

"Come on."

"Where?"

"It pays to be the boss," Styles answered. "I'll open the saloon early and we can each have a beer."

"Sounds good to me." Clint stood up too.

TWENTY-ONE

Wade Ballard knew he was no gunman. He had never killed a man in a fair fight in his life, except once, when he was nineteen. He had beaten a man to death then, but that had taken too much energy.

Ballard liked to consider himself a thinking man's killer. He never gave a victim an even chance to kill *him*, if he could kill the man from behind.

All of this meant that he certainly had no intention of facing the Gunsmith head on. That would be like committing suicide. The satisfaction would come in planning the killing, then successfully pulling it off. And that didn't even necessarily mean that he would pull the trigger himself. All he had to do was *cause* the death of Clint Adams, and Daryl Gaines would pay him a lot of money.

The first thing he had to do, then, was to figure out how he wanted to do it, and how many men he would need to pull it off.

Ballard had grown up with Daryl Gaines. He had known for years that Gaines was smarter than he was when it came to most things. But *killing* . . . well, Wade Ballard knew all about killing.

That's what Clint Adams, the Gunsmith, was going to find out.

In his office Daryl Gaines sat back in his chair and thought about Wade Ballard and Clint Adams. Take away Adam's famed gun and that would be some matchup. Of course, there was very little likelihood that Ballard would encounter Adams without his gun, so Ballard was going to have to use that special brand of animal cunning that made him such a good killer.

It was funny, Gaines thought, that as smart as he was—certainly smarter in most ways than Wade Ballard—he could not hope to match Wade Ballard's creativity when it came to killing. The man just seemed to have a natural talent for planning someone's death and then making it happen.

And, of course, that was why he used Ballard. Even as a child he had seen that side of Wade Ballard, had decided to use it and *had* used it to his advantage for years and years. And would for years to come.

TWENTY-TWO

Peter Styles had one beer with Clint in the saloon and then pleaded a busy work schedule. Clint decided to have a second beer. He nursed it while considering the situation he'd managed to get himself into.

He'd offered to help Toshiro Matsu in the beginning for one reason and one reason only— he was a nosy sonofabitch. He knew that. Lately, he'd been thinking that about himself a lot. It was probably the reason he *always* got involved in other people's problems. Oh sure, lots of times they were friends who asked for his help. But this time he had gotten curious about Matsu, and after stepping in to help him in the bar fight, had simply continued assisting him.

Now it looked as if he might be finding himself in the middle of a Japanese/Chinese conflict. Did he want any part of that? he asked himself. No. All he wanted to do was help Matsu find his traitors and the Emperor's Sword. If, when that was done, Lee and Matsu wanted to square off, they could do it without him.

Fine.

Clint stared down at the remnants of his second beer and decided not to finish it. He picked up the mug and carried it to the bar, where the bartender was getting his bar ready for the day.

"Here you go," he said.

"What's wrong with it?" asked the bartender.

"One and a half is my limit for this time of the day," Clint said.

"See you later?"

"Probably," Clint said. He waved and started to leave the saloon.

While Clint was having a beer with Styles in the hotel's saloon Toshiro Matsu was up in his room cursing himself for a fool. It was one thing to allow Clint Adams to become involved in his hunt. That made sense. He needed a guide in this strange land, and Clint Adams seemed to be perfect for that. Now, however, this odd man Nok Woo Lee was involved, a Chinese who did not look like a Chinese. However, he smelled like a Chinese, and he talked like a Chinese.

Matsu walked to the window and stared out. If he was home, on his own ground, he would need no one. He did not like the feel of being away from home, of trying to hunt on foreign land. He did not like relying on others.

He thought briefly about the man, Nok Woo Lee. He had watched the way the man moved, the way he walked. He knew that Lee would be a formidable opponent, so why did he feel it necessary to provoke him? To cast aspersions on his abilities?

Being here, away from home, away from his assigned duties, was affecting him badly. Why did he feel such anger all the time? Anger against the traitors, yes. That was understandable. But why did he feel anger toward the others? The people he passed in the streets? The man Styles, who was trying to help.

It was odd, but the only person he had not felt anger for since his arrival was Clint Adams. Here, he felt, was a man like himself, cast apart from the others by his abilities, by his reputation. They had much in common, he and the one they called the Gunsmith. They would work well together— that is, if Matsu himself could control his anger at all the others around him. If he did not allow his feelings to intrude on his working relationship with Clint Adams.

He had done it only recently. Upon arrival back at the hotel he had left Clint Adams standing in the lobby and had come directly up here. His anger had gotten the better of him, and he did not want the other man to see him when he was not in control.

Now, however—he took a deep, cleansing breath, filling his lungs and then letting it out slowly—now he felt in control once again.

Matsu decided that he had better find Clint Adams and apologize for his behavior. It was the honorable thing to do, and let no one call Toshiro Matsu anything less than honorable.

TWENTY-THREE

When Matsu came down to the lobby he knew that he drew stares, but he ignored them. He also tried to quell the rising tide of anger inside him. Ignoring the people who were staring, he walked directly to the front desk.

"Uh, yes, sir?" the clerk said, nervously. "Can I help you?"

"Mr. Adams," Matsu said. "Do you know where he is?"

"Uh, yes, sir, I do. He's, uh, in the saloon with Mr. Styles."

"Thank you," Matsu said politely.

As polite as he had been, however, he had terrified the clerk, who breathed a sigh of relief as the Japanese man walked off.

Matsu was about to enter the dining room and head for the saloon when he saw Peter Styles come out of the saloon. He stopped a moment to see where Styles would go. Instead of coming through the dining room, Styles changed direction and went through a door that looked like it led to the kitchen.

Matsu started through the dining room, drawing the attention of the few diners who were there at that time of day. He ignored them and walked to the entrance of the saloon. He saw Clint Adams sitting alone at a table, staring into a half-empty mug of beer. Matsu stood there a few minutes, watching his good friend, wondering what was going through the man's mind. Was he beginning to regret having offered his help to a stranger? Wishing he could walk away from it now?

Abruptly, Clint stood up and walked to the bar with the remainder of his beer. He exchanged a few words with the bartender, then turned to leave. He saw Matsu standing in the doorway.

"How long have you been there?" Clint asked.

"A short time," Matsu said. "What were you thinking about?"

"You," Clint replied, "and the whole situation."

"Do you wish to—how would you say it—back out? Is that right?"

"That's the way I'd say it," Clint said, "if I wanted to say it, which I don't. No, I don't wish to back out, Matsu. I wish to see this through to the end. Come on, let's go for a walk."

"Where?"

Clint shrugged. "Just a walk. I'll tell you what Peter Styles and I were just talking about."

Matsu was impressed. He had wondered if Clint would tell him that he had been talking to Peter Styles, or if he would have to bring it up himself by saying that he'd seen Styles come out of the saloon.

Matsu felt more and more that he and Clint Adams were very much alike.

As they walked around outside Clint replayed his conversation with Peter Styles, almost word for word where it concerned Matsu. He told him what Styles had said about the two traitors needing to sell the sword to the highest bidder.

"And he thinks that he can find out who they are selling it to?" Matsu asked.

"Well, Styles has some contacts in San Francisco," Clint said. "He may be able to find out who would try to help them with this. I mean, after all, we are talking about a stolen item, right?"

"Yes," Matsu said, "definitely."

"Okay, then," Clint replied, "they're not going to come here and start trying to sell the damn thing on the street. They're going to need a . . . a broker."

"And Styles can find him?"

"He can find some brokers who'd be likely to deal in merchandise like that," Clint answered. "After that I think it would be up to us to find the *right* one."

"We can do that," Matsu stated, with a nod of his head.

"Yes," Clint said, wondering if the man was indeed waiting for an answer, "yes, I think we can do that, all right."

They walked back to the hotel. Clint said, "You might want to get some rest."

"Why?"

"I'm going to take you out tonight."

"Where?"

"Out on the town," Clint said. "Show you a little bit of San Francisco."

"I do not think—"

"It's a condition of my continued help, Matsu," Clint said. "Everybody needs to relax sometime, and who knows if we'll get another chance to relax in the next few days. So . . . what do you say?"

Matsu studied Clint for a moment, then said, "You are my host. It would be impolite for me to refuse your invitation."

Clint frowned and said, "Well, that's not the most enthusiastic 'yes' I've ever gotten, but I think I'll take it."

TWENTY-FOUR

That night when Clint showed up at Matsu's room he was carrying some new clothes.

"What are these?" Matsu asked as Clint handed them to him.

"These clothes are a little better than the ones we bought for you before," Clint said. "These are what you'll wear when we go out tonight."

"I will put them on," Matsu said.

"Yes, you will," Clint said, "but *after* you do one other thing."

"What thing?"

"Take a bath?"

"A bath?"

Clint nodded. "Yes, a bath. Come on. . . ."

Clint waited outside while Matsu took a bath. When the Japanese man appeared he looked somewhat bedraggled. He had dressed in his new clothes, a dark suit that Clint had bought him. It fit pretty well, but the fact that his hair was still wet didn't help his overall appearance.

"Back inside," Clint said, pushing him.

"Wha—"

"We've got to dry that hair before you make a mess of these clothes."

Clint felt odd helping the man dry his long, thick hair. In the end it was still damp, but at least it wasn't dripping.

"There," Clint said. "Now let me look around here for something—here, comb your hair and then we can be on our way."

Matsu ran the comb through his hair, then turned for Clint's appraisal.

"That's fine," Clint said. "You still look like a warrior, but at least you look like a dressed-up warrior. I'll tell you one thing."

"What?"

"I think the ladies are going to like you tonight," Clint said.

"I have an interest in . . . ladies," Matsu said, gruffly.

Clint stood back and stared at the man.

"You're not married, are you?"

"No."

"Good," Clint said. "I wouldn't want to think that I was corrupting you, or making you cheat on your wife, or anything."

"That is silly," Matsu said. "I cannot be corrupted."

"Maybe not by money," Clint said, "but, my friend, some of the women you are going to see tonight could corrupt a priest."

Matsu made a sound like he was clearing his throat, and Clint took that as a sign of disapproval.

"Okay," Clint said, "I'm going to take a bath, and then get dressed, and then we can be on our way."

"Where shall I wait?"

"You'd better wait right outside in the hall, Matsu," Clint said. "I don't want to let you out in public looking like that unless I'm there to protect you."

Matsu said "Humph," and went outside to wait.

When Clint came out, dressed and dried, Matsu pushed himself away from the wall he was leaning against and looked at him.

"How do I look?" Clint asked.

Matsu frowned.

"I am not accustomed to commenting on the way men look," he said.

"Yeah, I know," Clint said, "me neither, but I think we both look pretty good. I think the ladies of San Francisco better look out tonight, don't you?"

"I do not think—"

"Okay, come on," Clint said, cutting him off before he could back out. "Let's get out there and enjoy the night. I get the feeling that tomorrow we'll be getting back to work."

"Good," Matsu said as Clint led him down the hall.

"What a grouch," Clint said.

TWENTY-FIVE

Clint expected stares, and he felt that he and Matsu could deal with that. What he didn't really expect—not in Portsmouth Square, anyway—was trouble.

The stares came, and they came early. Men stared at Matsu, and who knew *what* they were thinking. But it was different with the women.

Clint prided himself on knowing women—especially attractive women. He knew what an attractive woman was thinking when she looked at him a certain way, and he thought he knew what the women were thinking when they looked at Toshiro Matsu. Of course, when some of those women were with other men, he also knew what the men were thinking.

Matsu seemed to be oblivious to all the attention he was receiving. They went to several of the larger gambling establishments in the square. Matsu was no more interested in the people in these places than he was in the gambling.

"Okay, you win," Clint finally said to him at one point.

Matsu turned to him with a frown. They were in the famed Alhambra, watching the games.

"But . . . I am not playing anything."

"That's not what I meant," Clint said. "I mean that I'm tired of trying to show you a good time. Haven't you noticed any of the women we've seen tonight?"

"Of course I have seen them," Matsu said.

"Well, some of them would have liked it if you *acknowledged* that you had seen them."

"It is not my way."

"Don't you like women?" Clint asked.

"Yes," Matsu said, "I like women, but not when they are painted and preening."

Clint looked around the room at the women who were there. He had to admit that most of them *were* "painted and preening."

"I never looked at it that way," he said, morosely. "I think you just ruined it for me."

"I am sorry—"

"Never mind," Clint said, raising his hand. "Maybe we should just go back to the hotel and get some sleep."

"Yes," Matsu said, "maybe that would be best."

If they had made it out of the Alhambra they probably would have gotten back to the hotel without incident. Unfortunately, that wasn't to be.

As they started for the door a man moved into their path. He was pulling along with him a long-haired woman who was wearing a dress that she was more out of than in. Clint swore that if she bent over her generous bosom would have spilled right out.

"Excuse us," Clint said, and he and Matsu split to go around the couple.

"Hey, hold it," the man said. He reached out and grabbed Clint's arm, a move Clint didn't appreciate.

"Excuse me?" he said again, this time in a totally different tone.

Matsu also stopped and stared.

"I just wanna talk to you," the man said, taking his hand off Clint's arm. Clint could tell from the man's words—which were slurred—and his eyes—which were slightly out of focus—that the man was drunk. The woman, on the other hand, seemed sober and somewhat embarassed.

"What about?"

"My lady, here," he said, "she's interested in your pet gorilla."

"What?"

"You know, *him*," the man said, pointing his thumb at Matsu. "I mean, she thinks he's good looking, and I was tryin' to tell her that he ain't a man, he's a goddamned *gorilla*, right? I mean, he's big, an' he's got all that hair, he's got to be a—"

"You're drunk, friend," Clint said, taking a step closer to the man, "and your mouth is taking you someplace you don't want to go."

"Izzat so?" the man said.

The woman looked at Clint pleadingly and said, "I'm sorry, mister—"

Clint held his hand up to stop her. "It's not your fault, miss. Your friend has just had a little too much to drink."

"I have?" the man retorted, looking shocked. "What about my friends?" he asked.

"Who?"

"Those fellas there behind you," the man said, thrusting his jaw out to point the way.

Clint turned and looked behind him. There were three or four men clustered together, watching the proceedings, and they were grinning.

"They're with you?" Clint asked.

By now others had started watching, too. A ring had formed around Clint, Matsu, the drunken man and his woman friend.

"They sure are," the man said, grinning. "So you see, my mouth ain't startin' anythin' me an' my friends can't finish."

"You think that those men are going to come to your aid?" Clint asked.

"My *aid*?" the man mocked, widening his eyes. "My, my, my *aid*. Yeah, they're gonna come to my aid, friend."

"Why would they let your mouth get them into something they can't handle?" Clint asked.

"Ha!" the man said. "You don't think me and them can handle you and your pet gorilla?"

Clint looked past the man at a surprisingly calm Matsu—considering that it was *he* the man was insulting.

"Friend," Clint said, "I don't think you and your friends could handle *one* of us, let alone both of us."

"*One?*" the man said. "One of you? Which one?"

"Take your pick, big mouth."

The man turned and looked at Matsu. He must have seen something in the Japanese man's eyes that he didn't like.

"Well, I ain't about to fight no gorilla," the man said, grinning at Clint, "so I pick you."

Actually, Clint had been kind of hoping that Matsu would be the one who took care of the five men. After all, he had seen the Japanese handle five men before.

He looked around and saw the four other men separate themselves from the crowd that had gathered. Suddenly he realized that he had done just what he'd accused the drunken man of doing. He had let *his* mouth get him into something he was going to have to handle.

"How about outside—" he started, but he had no time to finish.

The drunken man suddenly pushed his lady friend away from him. She went staggering and would have fallen if Matsu hadn't encircled her waist with one thick arm.

Clint didn't see that, though. He was too busy ducking a clumsy roundhouse punch from her boyfriend. The punch whistled over his head. Clint then used one foot to sweep the man's *two* feet out from under him. As he fell to the floor Clint turned to face the other four.

He wondered for a moment if Matsu was going to help him.

TWENTY-SIX

The four men started for him at the same time. Clint sidestepped, moving all the way to his right. The two men on his left collided when they tried to change direction and were drunk enough that they knocked each other off balance.

Clint threw a left jab into the face of the man closest to him, deliberately aiming for the man's nose. It was a hard, straight punch, and the man's nose immediately started leaking blood. It might even have been broken.

As the man stopped and put both hands up to his nose, Clint reached for the lapels of the fourth man. Using his head he butted his adversary on the bridge of the nose. This time he knew he had broken the man's nose. He released the man, who staggered backwards. Now two men were standing there holding their noses.

The first two men had regained their balance by this time. Clint was now fully into the fight and ready for them. His breathing was measured, and he was actually enjoying himself.

He moved toward the two men and kicked out

quickly, catching one man right on the kneecap. The man cried out in pain and staggered. The second man stopped suddenly, as if he realized that he was the only one left.

"Come on," yelled the first man, the one who had started it all, "let's get him."

Clint turned quickly in the direction of the voice and saw the man charging him. He side-stepped, reached out, and grabbed his opponent by the lapels. Using the man's own force against him Clint propelled him directly into the other man. They collided painfully, banging heads, and both fell to the floor.

Clint turned quickly to see where the others were. They were all nursing their wounds, two with leaking noses and the other with a gimpy knee. He turned back to the last two, who were still sitting on the floor, dazed.

Clint turned and saw Matsu. His friend still had one arm around the woman, and they were both watching Clint.

"Where were you?" Clint demanded.

"I was right here," Matsu said. He slid his arm from the woman's waist and took a step away from her.

"Didn't it occur to you that I might need help?" Clint asked.

Matsu thought a moment, then said, "Yes, it did occur to me. But it was not the case, was it? Besides, they were very drunk."

"What's going on here?" a voice demanded. Several more men appeared on the scene, and Clint could tell that they worked for the hotel.

"These five men started a disturbance," Clint explained. Some of the other patrons chimed in their agreement.

"Wasn't his fault at all," one said.

"He tried to avoid it," another helpful person said.

The woman then stepped forward. She said, "It was all their fault. They got drunk and started a fight."

"With who?" one of the casino men asked.

"With him," she said, pointing to Clint.

The man looked at Clint. "You don't look like you've been in a fight," he said.

"He was magnificent!" the woman exclaimed. "They never touched him."

"Of course," Clint said, repeating Matsu's words, "they *were* very drunk."

"All right," one of the hotel men said to the others, "let's get them outside."

He looked at the woman. "Ma'am, you're with them?" he asked as his partners hustled the others out of the hotel and into the street.

She was at a loss for words when Clint stepped in. "No, she's with us."

"Is that right?" the hotel man asked her.

"Yes," Matsu said, "it is correct."

"Yes," she said with a smile, "I'm with them."

"All right," the hotel man said and followed his colleagues out.

They watched while the five troublemakers were escorted out. Clint then turned to the woman.

"What's your name?"

"Trudy," she answered. "Trudy Bennet."

"Well, Trudy, it looks like you're without an escort now."

"No, I'm not," she said, smiling. "I have two. Besides, I didn't come here with them, I just happened to meet one of them here. I didn't realize he would turn out to be a bad drinker, and a troublemaker."

Clint studied her and saw that she was younger than he had first thought, probably in her early twenties. She was full bodied, though, filling her dress to the point of bursting. Her hips were as round and firm as her breasts, and her legs were solid.

"Where are we going now?" she asked.

"Well," Clint started to say, "my friend and I were actually heading back to our hotel—"

"But," Matsu said, cutting him off, "perhaps we can go somewhere else and . . . do something."

Clint looked at Matsu. If he didn't know better he would have sworn the Japanese man was looking at Trudy Bennet's prodigious breasts.

TWENTY-SEVEN

Trudy Bennet looked down at the sleeping form of—she hoped she got this right—To-shir-o Matsu? Yes, that was it. She had decided, just before they went to bed, that she was going to call him "Mat." He didn't seem to mind it too much, especially when she was sitting astride him, his rigid penis buried up inside of her so deep that it felt as if it were nestled between her breasts.

"Oh yes, Mat, yes," she had said, touching herself between her breasts. "I feel like you're right up here!"

He had grunted, taken hold of her hips and turned her over. In that position he had spread her legs wide and proceeded to drive into her brutally. She had closed her legs, abruptly trapping him between her powerful thighs, and cried out each time he rammed himself into her.

She stared down at his sleeping form now, enjoying the way his long black hair settled over his shoulders and chest. She also liked the matt of chest hair he had. Not too much, just enough to rub against her nipples and make them feel sore.

In fact, she felt sore all over. She had never been
to bed with a Japanese man. She wondered if they
were all so . . . so *impossible* to wear out. Up to
now she had never met a man who could match
her stamina.

When she had first spotted Matsu in the
Alhambra the night before she couldn't help but
stare at him and wonder. The way he looked and
moved had reminded her of a wild animal, and
it had been her mistake to mention this to her
drunken escort. He had immediately christened
the Japanese man a "gorilla." In effect, the whole
fight was her fault.

When she and Matsu had left Clint Adams
in the saloon of The Clapton House and come
upstairs to his room she couldn't help but ask
him why he hadn't helped his friend when he
was fighting all those men.

"He did not need it," Matsu had said.

"He could have gotten hurt."

"I would not have allowed that to happen,"
Matsu had replied, shaking his head.

"He *was* very good, though, wasn't he?" she'd
asked, even as Matsu was removing her clothes.

"Yes, he was," Matsu had responded quietly.
She could tell from the look on his face that he
was impressed with his friend.

"Have you been friends a long time?" she'd
asked as she removed *his* clothes.

"No, not a long time," he had said, taking her
breasts in his big hands.

God, she hadn't met many men who could
actually *palm* her breasts. That excited her, and

at that point they stopped talking about Clint Adams and concentrated on each other. . . .

He stirred now, rolled onto his back and opened his eyes. He stared quietly at the ceiling, not moving and not speaking.

"Mat?"

He didn't respond. It was as if he didn't hear her, but how could that be? She was sitting right there in bed next to him.

"Mat?" she said again.

This time his eyes moved and he looked at her.

"Good morning," she said.

He grunted.

"You don't talk much, do you?" she asked, giggling.

She felt his hands on her, drawing her down onto his chest so that his chest hair rubbed against her nipples. It didn't matter then whether he talked to her or not. . . .

Down the hall Clint Adams was being awakened by a somewhat more aggressive Karen. A moment earlier she too had been sitting in bed staring down at the sleeping man next to her. But then she had decided to wake him herself rather than waiting for him to wake up on his own.

She had spread his legs and, nestling herself comfortably between them, proceeded to use her mouth to wake him up. Moments later she knew he was awake by the way he was breathing, but he kept his eyes closed and allowed her to continue to work on him. Finally he had groaned and reached for her, pulling her up on top of him.

She lifted her hips and took him inside, where she was very wet and hot. She pressed her hands down onto his chest and began riding him up and down, breathing heavily and moaning.

"Oh yes, oh yes, oh damn, oh yes," she muttered as she bounced up and down on him faster and faster and faster . . . and then finally, "Oh . . . God!" She bounced on him frantically, then collapsed atop him, both of them covered with perspiration.

"What happened to you last night?" Karen asked Clint later.

"What do you mean?"

"You were very keyed up when you got back," she said. She had been waiting for him in the saloon, and it was there that she had met him with Matsu and Trudy. They had gone up to Matsu's room first. Shortly thereafter she and Clint had gone to his room where, without delay, he had undressed, taken her to bed and delighted her with his eagerness.

He frowned. "I got into a fight with five drunks."

"Five?" she asked, her eyes widening. "Are you trying to impress me?"

"There's nothing impressive about fighting with drunks," he said. "They're at a distinct disadvantage from the start."

"But still . . . five men, and you're not even marked," she said.

"Don't be impressed," he said. "I saw Matsu take on five perfectly sober men the other night, in a Barbary Coast saloon, and they never touched him."

"That impressed you?"

"Yes."

"Then *he* must have been impressed with you last night," she said.

"I don't know . . ."

"He doesn't strike me as the kind of man you could ask," she said.

"No, he's not."

"Still," Karen continued, "you two seem to like each other."

He looked at her. "What makes you say that?" Truth be told, Clint couldn't tell with Matsu. He didn't know if the man liked him, or was just accepting his help out of necessity.

"I can tell by the way you are together," she said. "I've seen a lot of men, Clint, and believe me, you two like each other."

He looked at her, then leaned over and kissed her. "How about breakfast?"

"You go ahead," she said, touching his cheek. "I've got to get some sleep, remember? I'm a working girl."

He dressed, kissed her, told her he'd see her later, and went downstairs for breakfast.

TWENTY-EIGHT

Clint passed by Matsu's door on his way down the hall but restrained himself from knocking. There was no reason to disturb the man this early, especially if Trudy were still with him.

Clint was still somewhat surprised that Matsu had taken to Trudy. She was, after all, what he called "painted." He had to admit, though, she did have a body that gave a man ideas, and Toshiro Matsu was, after all, a man. Clint found it comforting that the man had given in to Trudy's charms. It made his friend seem more human.

Downstairs he found Peter Styles sitting at his usual table. Today, though, he was breakfasting on a plate of fresh fruit.

"Trying to lose weight?" Clint asked.

Styles looked up and said, "I like fruit. This getting to be a habit? People will say we're in love."

"I can go sit somewhere else, if you like," Clint offered.

"Shut up and sit down," Styles said.

Clint sat and regarded Styles's fruit platter with interest. When Felix, the waiter, came over he said, "I'll have the same."

"And coffee, sir?"

"Of course."

"Where's your friend this morning?" Styles asked.

"He's in his room," Clint said, "with a new friend."

Styles stopped eating and stared across the table at Clint.

"He likes women?"

"Apparently," Clint said, "and they like him."

"Will wonders never cease," Styles said. "Somehow I just didn't think he'd be interested in that. Anybody I know?"

"No," Clint said, "somebody we met at the Alhambra."

"Is she a pro?"

Clint thought a moment, then said, "I don't think so. I think she just . . . goes out a lot, and likes men. In fact, she was with five of them when we got there."

"Really? Did they give her up willingly?"

"No," Clint said but didn't elaborate.

Felix set the fruit platter down in front of him, poured him a cup of coffee and put the pot down on the table.

"Thanks, Felix."

Felix responded with a small bow that reminded Clint of Matsu.

"I don't suppose you found out anything yet?" Clint asked.

"I have some feelers out," Styles said. "I might get something back today."

"I just hope they're not gone by now," Clint said. "I'd like to wrap this up right in the city."

"And if they are gone?" Styles asked. "What will you do then?"

"Well . . . he'll want to go after them. I can't let him try to track them by himself. He'd never find them. In fact, he might get lost and no one would ever find *him*."

"Somehow I doubt that," Styles said wryly. "He strikes me as being more than able to take care of himself."

"I suppose so," Clint said, "but still . . ."

"I know," replied Styles. "You feel responsible for him, don't you?"

"Yeah, I guess I do," Clint said. "Why do you suppose that is?"

Styles shrugged. "Beats me. Maybe you're just too nice a man for your own good."

"Think so?"

"No."

They finished their fruit in silence.

TWENTY-NINE

Peter Styles had left Clint at the table to go to work. Clint was working on his second pot of coffee when Toshiro Matsu finally put in an appearance. The Japanese came to the entrance of the dining room, located Clint and walked over to him. Clint studied the man but could not have told by his appearance that anything unusual had occurred last night.

"Good morning, Matsu," Clint said. "Or should I call you Mat?"

Matsu winced at the sound of the bastardized version of his name. He sat down, leaving the chair recently vacated by Styles empty.

"Please," he said, still with a pained look, "do not call me that."

"I'm sorry," Clint said, with an amused look. "I didn't mean—"

"It is all right," Matsu said. "My actions last night warrant . . . ridicule."

"No," Clint said, "I wasn't ridiculing you, Matsu. I was . . . making fun, maybe . . . teasing you . . . but I'd never ridicule you."

Toshiro Matsu acknowledged the statement with a nod of his head, then looked up as the waiter appeared and asked what he would like for breakfast.

"What did you have?" the Japanese asked Clint.

"Fruit."

Matsu looked at Felix and said, "Fruit."

"And coffee?" Felix asked.

"Yes."

Felix nodded and left to fill the order.

"What happened to Trudy?" Clint asked.

"She went home," Matsu said.

"Are you going to see her again?"

Matsu did not look at Clint when he replied.

"I do not . . . think so."

Clint had the feeling that the man was originally going to reply, "I do not know," but then changed his answer midstream.

"Did you . . . sleep?" Clint asked. He was fighting to keep a smile off of his face.

"Yes," Matsu said, then added, "some." He kept his eyes averted. Clint realized that the man was genuinely uncomfortable with his behavior and decided to drop the matter completely.

"I've spoken with Styles this morning," Clint said. "He seems to feel he may have some information for us sometime today."

"That would be fortunate," Matsu said. "Anymore time wasted might put the traitors beyond our reach."

"They'd have to fly off the face of the earth to be beyond our reach, Matsu. Wherever they go, we can track them."

"I could not ask you to commit that much of your time—" Matsu started, but Clint cut him off.

"I have a failing, Matsu," he said.

"What is that?"

"I always finish what I start."

"You consider this a failing?"

"Well," Clint said, backing off a bit, "maybe we should call it a . . . trait."

"A better word, I think," Matsu said. "It is one I share."

Felix arrived with Matsu's fruit and they suspended conversation until he withdrew. Clint noticed that Matsu was wearing his sword on his back again. The only time he had seen the man without it was the previous night, while they were visiting the Portsmouth Square establishments. He did, however, have the smaller weapon with him then.

"You didn't have your sword with you last night," Clint said, "The big one, I mean."

"It is called a *katana*," Matsu said. "No, I carried the smaller blade. And you, you did not wear your gun."

That was true. But Clint had been carrying the little Colt New Line that he frequently used as a surprise weapon.

"I carried a smaller weapon, too," Clint said.

"I see we are very much alike," Matsu said, "in even more ways that I thought."

"I suppose that's true," Clint agreed. "We're both stubborn, I think, and finish what we start."

"We are both warriors," Matsu said. "You

proved that to me last night."

"With those five drunks?" Clint said.

"They were not *so* drunk that they could not have done you great harm," Matsu said.

"Well, you were there to back me up," Clint said. "I figured you'd step in if I needed help."

Matsu concentrated on his fruit and did not answer.

"I mean, just as I would have stepped in the other night if *you* needed help."

Again, no reply.

"I mean . . . I *think* you would have helped me . . . but I'm not *completely* sure . . ."

Matsu chewed on a piece of melon, then looked up at Clint and said, "Of course."

Clint stared at the man, who continued to eat his fruit. He still wasn't so sure.

THIRTY

"Mr. Gaines?" Althea Bonner said.

Daryl Gaines looked up from his desk and smiled at Miss Bonner.

"Yes, Miss Bonner?"

"Mr. Ballard is here."

"Good," he said, "let him in."

She nodded and backed away. Ballard entered and closed the door.

"Well?" Gaines asked. "Is it done?"

"No."

"When?"

"I've got it figured out," Ballard said. "Tonight, or tomorrow at the latest."

Gaines elevated his eyes. It looked as if he was looking at the ceiling, but he wasn't. He was looking at something only he could see.

"Does that fit into your plans?" Ballard asked. "Whatever they are?"

Gaines looked back at Ballard. "Just get it done, Wade."

Ballard smiled. "Don't worry. Whatever scheme you're working on, I'm not interested."

"You never are, Wade," Gaines said. "That's why we get along so well. You never ask questions."

"There's no need to," Ballard said, "when I don't care about the answers."

Ballard hadn't taken a seat, and now he turned and left the office. He left the door open behind him.

Gaines mentally reviewed his future plans. The two Japanese were ready to leave, and would do so in the morning. They were delivering the sword to the buyer themselves, and would collect their payment then. Gaines would be sending his own men with them, and they would in turn collect *his* fee. They would also protect the sword, or take it from the Japanese, whichever Gaines chose.

He hadn't really decided yet.

Ballard stopped at Althea Bonner's desk and smiled at her.

"Ready to change men, Althea?" he asked.

She smiled at him. "Would you treat me any better than he does, Wade?"

"Sure I would," Ballard answered. "Of course, he *does* have more money than I do."

"I'll weigh that fact when I make my decision, Wade," she said.

"You're a smart girl, Althea." He cupped her chin in his hand. "You'll do what's best for you."

"I always do, Wade," she said.

He grinned at her and left.

THIRTY-ONE

There wasn't much for Clint and Matsu to do except wait for either Styles or Lee to come up with something for them. Matsu decided to spend the time in his room. Clint had no way of knowing whether or not Trudy Bennet was there with him, but it really didn't matter. How Matsu spent the time was his business.

Clint decided to spend it in the saloon. He entertained the idea of joining a poker game that had begun at a corner table but decided against it. Instead he sat in the opposite corner, nursing a beer or two and relaxing as much as he could.

Late in the afternoon he noticed Peter Styles enter the saloon and look around. When he spotted Clint he came walking over.

"Where's Matsu?" Styles asked.

"In his room," Clint said. "Why?"

"There's somebody who wants to see you."

"Where?"

"In my office."

Clint stood up.

"I'll have someone go upstairs and get Matsu,"

Styles said. "You go on ahead."

"Thanks."

Styles's demeanor led Clint to believe that the person waiting for him in the office was Styles's friend, Nok Woo Lee.

He left the saloon and made his way to the office, entering without knocking. As he had surmised, Lee was sitting behind Styles's desk, drinking Styles's excellent sherry.

"Does Peter know you're drinking his sherry?" Clint asked.

"Why shouldn't I drink it?" Lee asked. He was more conventionally dressed than he had been when they first met. "I get it for him. Do you want a glass?"

"No, thanks," Clint said. "Do you have some information for me?"

"Where is your . . . Japanese friend?" Lee asked.

"He's on the way," Clint said. "He should be here any minute."

"Good."

"You're not going to antagonize him, are you?" Clint asked.

"Me?" Lee said, innocently. "It was he who antagonized me, last time."

"Perhaps it was, but—"

Lee held up his hand, cutting Clint off.

"Don't worry, Mr. Adams," Lee said. "If I want to antagonize Mr. Matsu, I'll wait until our business is concluded to do so."

"Well, do me a favor," Clint said, "don't do it while I'm around. I don't want to watch the two of you tear each other apart."

"I'd be interested in hearing who you would bet your money on," Lee said. He then added, "That is, if you were a betting man."

"I am a betting man, Mr. Lee," Clint said, "very frequently, in fact, but before I placed a bet I'd have to see you in action. I've already seen him."

"Impressive, is he?"

"Very."

Lee nodded.

"I thought he would be," he said. "It would be an . . . interesting contest."

"I don't doubt it."

At that moment the door opened and Toshiro Matsu entered the room. He moved to stand next to Clint, clasped his hands behind his back, and stared at Lee expectantly without speaking.

"Ah, Mr. Matsu, good," Lee said, sitting forward, "you're here."

"What have you got for us, Lee?" Clint asked.

"I've located your men," Lee said.

"Where?" Matsu asked.

"In Chinatown, as you suspected," Lee said, standing up.

"How did you find them?"

"It would be hard for two Japanese men, traveling together, to go unnoticed in Chinatown," Lee said. "I have many eyes and ears that I rely on. I've written the address down on a piece of paper." He pointed. "It's there on the desk."

He moved around them toward the door, and then stopped.

"I also wrote down my fee—my full fee, that is, minus what you've already paid. I trust you to pay the balance at your earliest convenience. Uh, will you be needing me to go in with you?"

Clint looked at Matsu, who shook his head almost imperceptibly.

"No, thank you," Clint said. "I think we'll handle this part ourselves."

"As you wish," Lee said. "If you should need my assistance again, you know where to find me."

Clint nodded, and Lee left the room. He turned and looked at Matsu.

"I do not trust him," Matsu said.

Clint moved around the desk and picked up the piece of paper.

"The fee looks fair," Clint said.

"If you say so," Matsu replied. "What about the address?"

"I know where it is," Clint said. He held the piece of paper out to Matsu, who waved it away.

"I will depend on you to get us there," Matsu said. "We should leave immediately."

"Yes," Clint agreed, "we should."

Since Matsu was wearing his *katana* and Clint, his gun, they agreed to leave right then and there.

Outside they ran into Styles.

"Did you see him?"

"Yes," Clint said. Matsu continued on to the lobby while Clint talked with Styles.

"Did he have what you wanted?"

"He did."

"Then you may not need what I get," Styles said.

"If you get it, hang onto it anyway," Clint said. "There's no telling how this is going to turn out."

"I'll be here," Styles said. "Uh, what about Lee and Matsu?"

"That's up to them."

"It *would* be interesting, Clint."

Clint dismissed the idea with a wave of his hand. "I don't think I care to find out what the outcome would be."

THIRTY-TWO

As they approached the address in Chinatown that Lee had given them, Clint put his hand on Matsu's arm to stop him.

"You better let me go in first."

"Why?"

"Because I have the gun," Clint said.

"They will not have guns," Matsu assured him.

"Okay, if they're there alone they won't have guns," Clint said, "but if they've got help, *they're* sure to have guns."

"Then you take care of the men with the guns," Matsu replied, "and I will take care of the others."

Clint frowned as Matsu started to walk. He put his hand on the man's arm to stop him again.

"You got some of those star things with you?"

"Star things?"

"Those . . . star knives you throw. The what-did-you-call-ems?"

"*Shuriken?*"

"Yeah, that's them," Clint said. "You got some of them with you?"

"Yes."

Clint nodded. "Okay, let's go, then."

They moved forward together and stopped in front of a building constructed of wood. It didn't look very sturdy, but Clint knew differently. These buildings in Chinatown were deceptively strong and sturdy.

"That's the front door," Clint said. "We're not going in that way."

"Why not?"

"Because they'd expect us to go in that way."

"They are not expecting us," Matsu said.

Clint looked at Matsu. "We have a better chance of coming out of this alive if we act like they do."

Matsu thought a moment, then said, "Yes, I see. What do we do then?"

"We look for another way in," Clint answered. "Another door, a window or . . ." He looked up.

"The roof?" Matsu asked.

"Yes," Clint replied. "The roof."

"I will try the roof," the Japanese said.

"How will you get up there?" Clint asked.

"Trust me," Matsu said, as he moved away from Clint quickly. Before Clint knew it, the man was gone from view.

"Where the hell did he go?" he asked aloud, scratching his head. He shrugged and moved off in the other direction, looking for a door or window.

He found an alley, and when he moved down it he found what he was looking for, a window with a broken pane. He listened at the window first and, when he heard nothing, reached in with his hand to find the latch. As it turned out, the window was not locked and he was able to open it easily and slip into the building.

Either there weren't many windows in the building, or they were blacked out, because inside it was dark. He turned and looked at the window he'd just climbed through and saw that the unbroken panes had been blacked out.

Clint drew his gun and waited for his eyes to adjust to the dark. After a few moments he was able to make out some silhouettes, enough so that he wouldn't bump into anything. He cautiously began to move around.

He shuffled his feet, in case there was something on the floor that might trip him up. He couldn't figure out why the building was totally dark if Matsu's two Japanese traitors were supposed to be there.

He stopped in his tracks and frowned. What if they weren't there? What if this was a trap, and they had been set up by Lee? After all, the man worked for money. What if someone had offered Lee more money to set them up than *they* were paying him to find the two Japanese traitors?

Damn it, he thought, now he wished he could warn Matsu—and where was he, anyway? Hadn't he found the roof by now? Or had he been unable to get up there? If that was the case, then it wasn't bad enough that this might be a trap, he was also in it alone.

For a moment he thought about going back to the window he'd used to get in. Then he heard something, and he knew it was too late.

He heard someone moving behind him, which meant that whoever it was, was between him and the window.

Clint crouched and turned, trying to see in the darkness. All he could see was a small square of light through the broken window pane. Since the window looked onto the alley, there was no sunlight coming through, only a little daylight, and not enough of that to help.

Suddenly, he heard somebody laughing. It was an eerie sound, coming out of the dark.

"Who's there?" Clint said. "Come on, what's going on? Show yourself."

"The men you are looking for are not here, Mr. Adams," a voice said. It was an Oriental voice, and the accent didn't sound anything like Matsu's. Clint assumed that the speaker was Chinese.

"Where are they, then?" he asked.

"They are gone," the disembodied voice said.

"Well," Clint said, "if that's really the case I guess there's not much point in my hanging around here anymore, is there?"

"No," the voice said, "but you will not be leaving, either."

"Are you going to stop me?" Clint asked. Where the hell was Matsu?

"*We* are going to stop you."

"We?" Clint asked. "How many of you are there?"

"Enough, Mr. Adams," the voice said. "Enough."

"Well," Clint said, "let's do it, then."

The same voice said something in Chinese—
at least, he thought it was Chinese—and then he
heard some movement as more than one person
started coming towards him. In fact, it sounded
as if they were all around him.

Great, he thought, I'm surrounded and Matsu's
up on the roof somewhere, trying to find his way
in!

THIRTY-THREE

"Well, come on, then," Clint said.

No answer, but he could hear them coming, shuffling forward. Were they all Orientals?

"If you're going to kill me anyway," he said, "the least you could do is tell me who hired you."

Again, no reply.

He felt something behind him, whirled quickly and lashed out with the gun. He felt the barrel strike someone, and there was a grunt of pain. He lunged forward and grabbed the man. He was small and wiry, probably Chinese. He held him in front of him, left arm across his chest pinning the man's arms to his side, right hand held up high with his gun.

"Come on!" he shouted. He had a shield, now, in case they decided to start shooting.

Someone rushed him, slamming into him and the man he held. The three of them went down in a heap, and Clint rolled away frantically, making sure he held onto his gun rightly.

He had already decided that he wouldn't just fire into the dark, not while no one else was firing. There was still a chance he could get out of this, and he wanted someone alive to answer some questions.

That changed, though, when someone lashed out at him, slicing open his left arm with a knife.

"Shit!" He pointed and fired his gun. As the muzzle flashed he saw the man's face briefly, twisting in pain as the bullet invaded his body.

Things happened quickly then. He heard them happen, but couldn't see it.

Someone grunted, another man screamed, and yet no one charged him again. Maybe his gun had frightened them off? But if they were there to kill him, why didn't they have guns?

Someone screamed, and he felt something wet splash on him. He wiped at his clothes with his hand and smelled blood, either his own or someone else's.

And then suddenly, there was nothing, just quiet.

"What's going on?" he called out.

Clint waited. He heard someone moving in the darkness but held his fire. Abruptly, he heard a scratch, and then a match flared. In the glow he saw the face of the man holding it.

It was Matsu.

"Let's find a lamp," he said to the Japanese.

They found one just as the match went out. Matsu lit another one and then lit the lamp. Suddenly everything was clear.

There were five men lying on the floor. One had a hole in his chest from Clint's bullet. Another was slashed from throat to belly, and

Clint needed only to look at the bloody sword in Matsu's hand for an explanation. He looked down at himself. He was covered with the dead man's blood, which had washed over him when Matsu had slit the man open. Also, Clint's left arm was leaking some blood of his own.

A third man lay on the floor, his head at an odd angle that indicated a broken neck.

The other two men looked unhurt, unmarked.

"We needed one alive," Clint said.

Matsu indicated the two unmarked men and said, "They are alive."

"Good," Clint answered. "Let's keep them apart and question them separately."

Matsu nodded. He leaned over to wipe his blade clean on the leg of one of the dead men and replaced the sword on his back. He leaned over, grabbed one of the unconscious men under the arms and dragged him to the other end of the room.

The building they were in was obviously some sort of warehouse. There were crates stacked against the wall, but the center of the floor was empty. Clint had a feeling the crates had been moved and stacked to make room for this trap.

From across the room Matsu's voice came out of the dark. The storm lamp was on the floor next to Clint's foot, and the light did not extend that far. That was good. When Clint's man woke up he wouldn't be able to see his unconscious cohort. He would, however, see the other three men, who were dead. In fact, Clint dragged the man over to the one Matsu had killed with his sword. He wanted that to be the first thing the man saw when he woke up.

"It was a trap."

"Yes."

"Set by that man Lee."

"Maybe."

"I say yes."

"We'll ask him," Clint said, "after we're finished here."

"Yes," Matsu said, "I will ask him."

Clint holstered his gun and examined the wound on his left arm. The knife had cut him cleanly but not very deep. It was bleeding, but it wasn't serious.

The man at his feet stirred.

Clint leaned down and took hold of the man's hair. As the Oriental's eyes fluttered open Clint held his head so that he was looking at the dead man's gaping wound.

"Aieee!" the man screamed when he saw the dead man's intestines.

"See that?" Clint said. "That's what happens to you if you don't answer my questions."

The man gave him a vacant, terrified look.

"Come on," Clint said, "you understand me, and you speak English."

The man continued to stare at him.

"All right," Clint said. He released the man's hair and stood up. He drew his gun and pointed it at him. "If you can't understand English, you're of no use to me."

"No, no, no," the man stammered, holding

his hands out, and then, "yes, yes, yes, I speak English."

"Look around you," Clint said.

The man looked around and saw the other two dead men lying on the floor.

"Who hired you?"

"I do not know."

"Wrong answer," Clint said, and cocked the hammer on his gun.

"I swear, I swear, I do not know. Only Chan knows," the terrified man answered.

"Which of these is Chan?" Clint asked.

The man looked at the three dead men and then back at Clint.

"They are not Chan? Where is he?"

That made the fifth man, the one Matsu had, Chan.

"Chan was your leader?" Clint asked.

"Yes," the man said, "he made the arrangements."

"Okay," Clint said, "that means I don't need you anymore."

The man took that to mean that Clint was going to kill him. He screamed, a sound which Clint cut off by pistol whipping him, one slash across the head that put him to sleep.

He picked up the lamp and walked towards Matsu.

"This is the man with the information," he said.

The man at Matsu's feet was stirring.

"I will make him talk," Matsu said.

Clint nodded, held the lamp and watched.

Matsu produced his sword again and as the man came awake he cut him under the chin.

"*Aieee!*" the Chinese man screamed, covering his chin with his hand.

"You will tell us who hired you," Matsu said.

"I cannot," the man said.

"Then you will die," Matsu said, "but slowly." And he cut him again, this time on the forehead. Clint did not even see the slash that opened the cut.

Blood poured down into the man's eyes, and he tried to wipe it away.

"I will be killed," the man shouted.

"I will kill you anyway," Matsu said. The sword moved faster than Clint's eyes could follow, and there was a finger lying on the floor. It was the little finger of the man's left hand.

The Chinese stared at his bloody hand in horror, until the blood from his forehead blinded him. He wiped at his eyes frantically. It seemed that the blindness frightened him more than anything else.

"Yes, yes, all right," he said, quickly. "Ballard, the man's name is Wade Ballard."

Matsu stepped back, taking a moment to wipe his blade on the man's pants. When the man felt that he jumped and screamed.

"Okay," Clint said to the man, "where do we find Wade Ballard?"

THIRTY-FOUR

Matsu wanted to kill the two remaining Chinese ambushers. Clint managed to dissuade him, though not easily. Actually, he had toyed with the idea of letting the Japanese man go ahead, but in the end had decided against it. It was too cold-blooded.

Chan told them where he was to meet with Wade Ballard, and when they left the building that was where they headed. The location was a saloon on the Barbary Coast. Clint and Matsu almost seemed to be going full circle, back to where they had first met.

"How did you get inside?" Clint asked as they headed for the Coast.

"By the roof."

"I didn't hear anything."

Matsu looked at him with heavy-lidded eyes. He said, "Neither did they."

"No, I guess not," Clint said. "How did you manage to move so surely in the dark?"

"I used my instincts," the Japanese man replied. "My ears, my nose . . ."

126

"You smelled them?"

"Yes."

"Amazing."

"Not really," Matsu said. "You have instincts, do you not?"

"Well, yes . . ."

"And they have kept you alive all these years?"

"Yes."

"It is the same thing."

"Somehow," Clint said, "I don't think so."

Matsu said no more about it.

"How did you get up to the roof, anyway?" Clint asked after a few moments.

"It does not really matter," Matsu said. "It is over, is it not?"

"Yeah," Clint said, "it's over. I'd just like to know how you managed it all."

"I managed it," Matsu said. "That is all that matters."

"If you say so," Clint said, giving up.

"This man Ballard," Matsu asked, "you have heard of him before?"

"No," Clint said, "never. Maybe Styles has heard of him."

"I do not trust Styles."

"Matsu—"

"It was Lee who sent us to that building to be killed," Matsu said, "and it was Styles who sent us to Lee."

"That's logical, of course," Clint said, "but it's not necessarily the truth."

"We will ask them," Matsu said. "After we finish with this man Ballard, we will ask them."

"All right," Clint said. "I'm all for asking them—but maybe we can keep them in one piece while we do it?"

Matsu didn't reply.

"I mean . . . not slice them up?"

No reply.

"Well," Clint finally said, "maybe just a nick . . . here and there . . ."

THIRTY-FIVE

"Okay," Clint said when they were across the street from the Seafarer's Saloon, "I really think I ought to go in alone this time."

"No."

"Listen to me," Clint said. "Don't be so stubborn without listening."

Matsu frowned and then nodded.

"If we walk in and he sees you, it's a dead giveaway," Clint explained. "He might go for his gun and then we'll have to kill him. We won't find out *anything* that way, Matsu. In order for him to tell us where your men are, and the sword, we've got to make sure we take him alive."

Matsu listened, thought it over and then nodded grudgingly.

"What do I do?"

"Go around the back," Clint said. "Get in that way, and wait for me to get the drop on him."

"Get the drop?" Matsu questioned.

"Have him covered with my gun," Clint hastily explained.

"All right," Matsu said.

"I'll give you five minutes to get set."

Matsu nodded and slipped away.

Clint waited the required time, then crossed the street and entered the saloon.

It was early in the day and there were only three men in the place. One of them fit Chan's description. He was sitting at a table against the back wall, playing solitaire. There was a half-full beer mug near his left hand. Clint watched as he dealt out the cards, noticing that he was right-handed. His gun would be on his right side.

Clint ordered a beer, then turned and sort of lazily took the room in. He moved slowly, so as not to attract too much attention. He started across the room and knew that the man had spotted him, even though he had not stopped dealing out his cards.

"Solitaire your only game," Clint asked, "or are you interested in poker?"

The man looked up at him, studying him for a moment before replying.

"I play poker," he said, "but not two-handed. It's a boring game, and it usually comes out even no matter how long you play."

"You're right," Clint said, putting his beer mug down on the table. "I've got another game that might interest you, though."

"Oh? What's it called?"

"Staying alive," Clint said. "Ever hear of it?"

Ballard frowned, puzzled but not yet suspicious.

"Can't say I have."

"Here's how you play," Clint said. "You put

the cards down and set your hands down flat on the table, where I can see them."

Now the man knew something was up.

"Don't go for your gun," Clint said. "You'll never make it."

"Who are you?" the man asked.

"I think you know the answer to that."

He could see by the look on the man's face that Clint's identity had suddenly dawned on him.

"Adams?"

"That's right," Clint said. "Set the cards down, and put your hands flat."

"And the Japanese?" Ballard asked, complying with the instructions.

"He'll be here any minute, Ballard," Clint said. "Your men were kind of sloppy. Most of them got killed."

"Not enough, obviously," Ballard said.

"No," Clint said, "you're right. Chan was able to tell us where to meet you. Sit easy, now. I'm going to take your gun. Don't make me kill you."

"Don't worry," Ballard said.

Clint moved around the table and carefully removed the man's gun from his holster. As he did so the back door opened and Matsu came in. He drew the attention of the other two patrons in the place and the bartender as he crossed the floor to Ballard's table.

Ballard looked at him and didn't say anything.

"All right, Ballard," Clint said. "We want to know where the sword is."

"What sword?" Ballard asked.

"The Emperor's Sword," Matsu said.

Ballard looked at Matsu. "What emperor? I don't know what you're talking about."

"Don't get him mad, Ballard," Clint said. "I've seen him use his sword."

"He can use it all he wants," Ballard said. "I don't know what the hell you're talking about."

Matsu brought his sword out from behind his back, but Clint touched his arm to stop him from doing anything rash. At the same time he studied Ballard.

"He's telling the truth," he said, finally.

"He is lying!"

"No," Clint stated, "he's telling the truth. He doesn't know about the sword."

"That's right," Ballard said. "I don't."

"You're working for someone, though," Clint said. "Somebody sent you after us."

Ballard didn't respond.

"Who is it, Ballard?" Clint asked. "Who do you work for?"

Again, Ballard didn't reply.

"I warned you about his sword," Clint said. "I can't control him when he starts using the sword. Pieces will start flying all over."

"He can shove his sword up his—" Ballard started, with no fear on his face or in his tone, but he stopped short as Matsu whipped his sword around with amazing speed.

Clint heard the blade cut through the air, and then something fell to the floor. Both Clint and Ballard looked down to see what it was.

It was an ear.

Ballard's right ear.

Slowly, in disbelief, Ballard lifted his right hand to his ear—only it wasn't there. It was on the floor. His hand came away bloody. His face was white with shock, but there didn't seem to be any pain—yet.

"What the—" Ballard said.

"It's started, Ballard," Clint said. "Save yourself a lot of pain."

"You—you're crazy!" Ballard said. He finally looked frightened. "Both of you!"

"That's one, Ballard," Clint said, slowly, pointing to the ear that was lying on the floor. "Do you want to try for two?"

THIRTY-SIX

Once again it was Clint who kept Matsu from killing.

"Next time," Clint told Wade Ballard as he and Matsu left, "he won't stop at an ear."

As they left Ballard was desperately trying to staunch the flow of blood from the spot where his ear used to be. At the door Clint turned and saw the man looking down at his ear, still on the floor, disbelief on his face.

"We should have killed him," Matsu said, outside. "He will come after us."

"Things are moving quickly, Matsu," Clint said. "By the time he decides to come after us we'll have this whole thing settled."

"Do you know this man he spoke of?" Matsu asked. "Daryl Gaines?"

"No," Clint said, "but maybe before we talk to Gaines we should have a conversation with Peter Styles."

"Why?"

"Gaines has his office on Market Street," Clint said. "Also, he's got money. I'd like to know what else he's got, and Styles is the man to tell us."

"Ballard will warn him," Matsu said.

"We'll make a quick stop," Clint said. "He'll take a little while to recover from losing his ear. We have some time."

The look on Matsu's face said that he didn't totally agree with everything Clint was saying, but he was willing to go along.

"Come on," Clint said, "let's get over to The Clapton House."

When they reached the hotel they went directly to the front desk.

"Where's Styles?" Clint asked the clerk.

The man looked up. When he saw both Clint and Matsu—two men he was afraid of, standing there together—he swallowed hard and backed away a few steps.

"Come on, come on . . . ," Clint said impatiently.

"He-he's in his office."

Both Clint and Matsu went around the desk. The clerk moved to one side to get out of their way quickly. They walked rapidly down the hall to the office door and entered without knocking.

Styles looked up from his desk and said, "What the—" as he started to rise.

"Sit down, Peter," Clint said. "You've got some explaining to do."

Styles, who had been halfway out of his chair, settled back into it and stared at the two men curiously.

Clint fronted the desk while Matsu moved

alongside it, standing to Styles's right.

"What's going on, Clint?" Styles asked. "What are you talking about?"

"I'm talking about a trap," Clint said. "It looks like your friend Lee sent us into a trap we weren't supposed to walk away from."

"He's not my man," Styles said. "He's just somebody that I . . . employ from time to time."

"I see," Clint said. "So you had no idea he was going to turn on us."

"Clint," Styles said, "Lee works for money. Somebody must have paid him more than you did."

"Like Daryl Gaines?"

Styles frowned. "What do you know about Daryl Gaines?" he asked.

"Not much," Clint replied. "Why don't you tell me something about him?"

"He's rich, and he has political aspirations," Styles said. "Mainly, he's relying on his father-in-law to get him into politics."

"What does he do?"

"Well, supposedly he's a lawyer, but it's funny you should come up with his name."

"Why?"

"He's one of the names I came up with as someone who might broker the stolen sword," Styles said. "Apparently he deals in stolen articles on the side."

"Maybe he's a lawyer on the side," Clint offered.

"That could be," Styles agreed. "Honestly, Clint, if Lee sent you into a trap I had nothing to do with it. What would I have to gain?"

"I don't know," Clint said. "What do you know about Wade Ballard?"

Styles looked surprised.

"Ballard? Where did you—"

"It was him who set the trap," Clint said. "He was working for Gaines."

"Well," Styles said thoughtfully, "that fits. They grew up together, and some say that Ballard does . . . odd jobs for Gaines."

"Odd jobs? Like murder, maybe?"

"Maybe," Styles said.

"No maybe about it," Clint said. "He set it up and was being paid by Gaines for the job."

"How do you know this?"

"He told us."

"Why would he?"

Clint stared at Styles pointedly and said, "Because he didn't want to lose his *other* ear."

THIRTY-SEVEN

"This is too easy," Clint said as they came to Daryl Gaines's building.

"What?" Matsu asked.

Clint turned to face the Japanese man. "This has all been too easy."

"We could have been killed in Chinatown today," Matsu said.

"But we weren't," Clint said.

"What is your point?"

"I don't know if I have one," Clint answered. He looked up at the second floor window that had Gaines's name on it. "This just seems too easy, that's all."

"We should go up," Matsu said. "I will get him to tell us where the sword is."

"Let's go," Clint said.

Even as they ascended the stairs Clint's mind was working. If this were the way it came out, with Gaines telling them where they could find the sword and the two thieves, then it really *was* too easy. Maybe, Clint thought, this is all just to keep us busy while the thieves put some distance between themselves and San Francisco. If that were the case, then it was working.

Upstairs they found themselves facing a lovely woman seated at a desk, who looked up at them first expectantly, then curiously.

"Can I help you?" Althea Bonner asked.

"We'd like to see Mr. Gaines," Clint said.

"Do you have an appointment?"

"No," Clint said, "but tell him that Mr. Wade Ballard sent us to see him."

"Wade . . . Ballard?" the woman said.

"Yes," Clint said. Then he asked, "You know Mr. Ballard, don't you, miss?"

"Uh . . . excuse me for one minute, please?" she said, getting up. She walked to a door, opened it and hurried through.

"If there is another door," Matsu said, "he could escape."

"I don't think so," Clint said. "I mean, he could, but I don't think he will."

"Why not?"

"This man is a pillar of the community, Matsu," Clint said. "He's a lawyer, he has political ambitions. I don't think he'll run. I think he'll just try to talk his way out of this."

"He will not succeed," Matsu said.

"Just do me a favor," Clint said.

"What?"

"Don't bring out your sword unless I say so, all right? Let's just try talking to him first."

"What good will that do?"

"Well, rather than go against us and risk his position," Clint said, "there's a possibility that he might just *give* us the sword, and your thieves."

"Why would he do that?"

"He'd be cutting his losses," Clint said. "It's the kind of thing a man like him would do."

"Cutting his losses?" Matsu asked, frowning.

"He'd rather lose his commission for selling the sword then lose his position and his reputation. And whatever chance he has at entering politics."

"I understand," Matsu said, although Clint had the feeling that the man didn't totally understand.

"Just trust me on this one, Matsu," Clint said. "Let me do the talking, all right?"

"All right."

They looked up as the door opened and the woman came out again. She did not bother to close the door behind her before she spoke.

"Gentlemen, Mr. Gaines will see you now. Right in here, please."

"Thank you," Clint said, smiling at her, "thank you very much."

THIRTY-EIGHT

When Clint and Matsu entered the room the man behind the desk stood up, looking unconcerned, and actually extended his hand for a handshake.

"Gentlemen," Daryl Gaines, "a pleasure. I understand you were referred to me by my friend, Wade Ballard?"

"Sit down, Mr. Gaines," Clint said, closing the door behind them.

"What?" Gaines said, looking puzzled. He withdrew his hand and said, "I'm sorry?"

"Sit down and stop playing your part so well," Clint said. "You know very well why Ballard sent us. He told us all about it."

"All about what?" Gaines asked.

Clint walked right up to the desk with Matsu close behind him. He stared hard at Daryl Gaines and said, "Do yourself a favor and sit . . . down."

Gaines, staring back at Clint boldly, nevertheless sat down.

"Perhaps you gentlemen will tell me why you're here?" he said.

"That's easy," Clint replied. "We want the sword."

"The sword," Gaines said. "Now what sword would that be, exactly?"

"The Emperor's Sword," Clint replied.

"Oh, well," Gaines said, "that explains everything, doesn't it?"

"Mr. Gaines," Clint explained, "my friend here has a sword of his own, see? Turn around and show Mr. Gaines your sword, Matsu."

The Japanese man turned so Gaines could see the sword.

"This is Toshiro Matsu," Clint said. "He was sent here specifically by the Emperor of Japan to retrieve the stolen sword. He was also sent to exact vengeance against the men who stole it."

"That's very interesting."

"It gets better," Clint continued. "The next time you see Wade Ballard ask him what happened to his right ear."

"His right . . . ear?" Daryl Gaines asked, not sure that he had heard correctly.

"That's right."

Gaines looked from Clint to Matsu. "You cut off Ballard's ear?"

"Like a hot knife going through butter." Clint spoke for Matsu. "You should have seen it. Ballard didn't even realize it was gone until he saw it lying on the floor."

Clint thought he saw the confident look on Daryl Gaines's face waver a bit. "Then there's the five men Ballard sent after us," Clint said. "One of them ended up cut from here to here." Clint pointed first to his throat and then to his belt buckle. "Another lost a finger before he decided to give us Ballard. It came off clean as could be."

"Mr. . . . ?"

"Oh, come on, Gaines," Clint said. "All right, just for the record I'm Adams, Clint Adams."

"Adams," Gaines said. "Mr. Adams . . . the Gunsmith, right?"

Clint didn't reply.

"Mr. Adams, are you trying to frighten me? Because if you are—"

"I'm not trying to frighten you, Gaines," Clint said. "I'm trying to help you."

"Oh? And how's that?"

"I'm trying to keep you from having to face this man and his sword."

Clint watched as Gaines flicked his eyes over to Matsu and then back to him quickly.

"You're trying to help me." It was a statement, not a question.

"I'm trying to help everyone, Gaines," Clint said. "I want Matsu to get the sword back, and I want you to stay alive. After all, I understand you're interested in a career in politics. You have to be *alive* for that."

"He wouldn't kill me," Gaines said.

"*Look* at him, Gaines," Clint said. "He's serious about this. Look at his face and tell me you don't think he would kill you."

Gaines stared at Matsu longer this time before looking back at Clint.

"That—that wouldn't help him get the sword back," Gaines stammered.

"If you're not going to help him," Clint said, "then he's got no reason to keep you alive."

"You—" Gaines started, then stopped, cleared his throat and started again. "You wouldn't let him kill me."

"I don't think I'd be able to stop him, Gaines," Clint replied. "I really don't."

Gaines looked away from them now, visibly shaken. Clint could see he was trying to come to a decision.

"You want some advice, Gaines?" he asked.

Gaines looked at him. "What?"

"Cut your losses," Clint offered. "Forget whatever it is you were going to make for brokering that sword. Tell us where it is, and we'll go and get it. It's as simple as that."

Gaines began to drum his fingers on the desk top while he thought, but when he noticed Matsu looking at the fingers he made a fist and drew it into his lap quickly.

"Come on, Gaines," Clint said. "Make a move, and make it the right one."

"I—I'm not going to admit anything, you understand," Gaines said. "I—I can't—"

"Just tell us what you want to tell us," Clint said.

"There's a man, a rancher in Nevada, outside of Stone City. He—he buys a lot of things like—like swords—"

"What's his name?"

"Burke."

"Full name."

"Henderson Burke," Gaines said. "The Bar-HB

ranch, near Stone City, Nevada."

"Has that sword left San Francisco?"

Gaines looked at Clint and cleared his throat.

"*If* I was going to sell something like that to Burke," Gaines said, "I would have sent it on its way this morning—a few hours ago."

"A few hours head start," Clint said, thoughtfully. He looked at Matsu. "That doesn't sound too bad."

Matsu didn't reply. He was staring hard at Daryl Gaines, while Gaines was doing his best to avoid the black stare of the Japanese man.

"All right," Clint said. "We have to get you a horse and get on our way."

He looked back at Gaines. "If we get to Stone City and find out that Henderson Burke got a telegraph message, we're going to come back here."

"He—he won't . . . ," Gaines said miserably.

"Let's go," Clint said to Matsu. He started for the door and realized that Matsu was still standing in front of Gaines's desk. "Matsu, he's just the broker. He didn't take the sword. We know where your thieves are, so let's go and get them."

Matsu stood stock still for a minute or two more, then slowly turned and walked to the door.

"Oh, one more thing, Gaines."

"What?"

"If you sent that sword to Nevada, would you send it with an escort?"

"Of course . . . ," Gaines said, looking away.

"You'll do well in politics, Gaines," Clint said. "You just learned to cut your losses. That's an important thing to know."

They went outside and closed the door behind them. The woman behind the desk looked up curiously.

"Your boss is not in a very good mood," Clint said. "Maybe you should take the rest of the day off."

She looked at the door, then back at Clint.

"Is he . . ."

"Oh, he's not hurt," Clint said, "or dead. He's just very disappointed with himself."

She looked at the door, then back at Clint once more. A smile tugged at the corner of her lips. She said, "Well . . . good."

THIRTY-NINE

Clint had left his big black gelding, Duke, at a livery stable near The Clapton House. He took Matsu there and together they picked out a horse for the Japanese to ride. The stable man did not have an animal the caliber of Duke, but the big Morgan that they picked out seemed to fit the bill.

They took the horses back to the hotel with them. Clint went in to talk to Styles again while Matsu arranged for a few supplies.

"Not too much," Clint said. "We're going to have to ride light if we're going to make up the three-hour head start they have on us."

"All right."

Clint went into the hotel and up to the desk clerk.

"Is he in his office?" he asked.

"Y-yes sir," the clerk asked, automatically stepping aside to allow Clint access to the hallway.

Clint went to the door of Styles's office. This time he knocked. Styles called out for him to come in. The hotel manager looked up from his desk as Clint approached.

"I wanted to talk to you again without Matsu around," Clint said.

"Clint," Styles said, spreading his hands, "I don't know how I can convince you that I had nothing to do with that ambush. All I did was send you to Lee."

"You can see how it looks, Peter."

Styles took a deep breath, held it briefly and then let it out.

"Yes, I can see how it looks," he said finally.

"So I'll just need your word on it, one last time, and then we'll drop it."

"You have my word, Clint," Styles said. "In fact, I'll be talking to Lee myself about it. If it's true, I won't be using him anymore, myself."

Clint nodded. "Matsu and I will be leaving very soon," he said.

"You know where the sword is?"

"If Gaines was telling the truth, and I think he was," Clint said. He explained to Styles his theory about Gaines cutting his losses.

"It makes sense," Styles said. "It also makes sense that the buyer would be outside San Francisco. I wish you luck. Will you be coming back here afterwards?"

"Yes," Clint said, "but probably to pick up my belongings and leave. It's time to get moving again, anyway."

"Well . . . ," Styles said, "I'll see you then."

As Clint left the man's office he knew that both he and Styles realized that their friendship, which had been growing, had come to a screeching halt because of the ambush.

When Clint got back the last thing he would do was go and see Lee and get that cleared up. He didn't want to leave any ends untied when he finally left San Francisco.

After Clint left his office, Peter Styles sat back in his chair and spent a long time thinking the situation over. He certainly did not have anything to do with the attempt on Clint Adams's life, but he didn't like the idea that Lee—a man he had recommended—might have. If indeed Lee had set Clint up, Styles could understand how Clint Adams would have difficulty ever trusting *him* again. This was evidenced by the fact that Clint had not even offered a clue as to where he was going to retrieve the sword.

FORTY

Clint had a rough idea where Stone City, Nevada, was and knew there was no chance they'd catch up to the thieves that day or even the next day. So there was no reason to push the horses all that much, at least not yet.

He was impressed with Matsu as a rider. The man moved with the horse as if they were one, and he left no question as to who was the master.

As for Duke, the black gelding was very happy to be out of a stall and back on the trail. The big horse liked nothing better than to run, and he had been cooped up a long time in San Francisco. However, Clint had to keep a tight rein on him because Matsu's Morgan could not keep up with him.

They rode until darkness started to fall and then made camp. All they had in the way of supplies were the makings of coffee and some beef jerky. Clint had survived for days on less, and he imagined that Matsu had also, many times.

There was something different about Toshiro Matsu now that the hunt had taken them away from the city and they were out on the trail. The hunt seemed to invigorate the man, and he seemed almost larger, somehow, if that were possible. Clint knew that he would probably cut an even more impressive figure if he were wearing his ceremonial clothing.

While they were unsaddling the animals Matsu openly admired Duke.

"He is a magnificent animal," he said. "A fitting mount for a warrior."

It didn't seem necessary for Clint to warn Matsu not to try to touch Duke. For the moment, Matsu was content to examine Duke's contours without touching him. A few moments later, though, when the Japanese reached with a big hand to touch the black gelding, Duke did a strange thing. He remained still and allowed Matsu to touch his massive neck. Clint could count on the fingers of one hand the number of people Duke had let touch him without trying to take one of their fingers off.

"Remarkable," Matsu said, stroking Duke's neck.

"More than you know," Clint said. "Duke *never* allows anyone to touch him."

Matsu looked at Clint and said, "He is a warrior's horse, and I am a warrior. He knows this."

"If you say so," Clint said. "I'll go and build us a fire for coffee."

By the time Matsu had finished picketing his own horse for the night Clint had the fire going and the coffee almost ready. When the Japanese warrior hunkered down next to the fire Clint handed him a piece of beef jerky. They each chewed in silence while they waited for the coffee to be ready. When it was they sat back with a cup of coffee each and finished their jerky.

"Tell me something," Clint said, then.

"What?"

"When we get where we're going," Clint said, "and your thieves are there, and the sword, what will you do?"

"I will take the sword back," Matsu said.

"And?"

"And I will have justice."

"For yourself?"

"For my Emperor," Matsu said, frowning. "I seek no justice for myself."

"What about vengeance?"

"That, too, is the Emperor's."

"Nothing for yourself, Matsu?"

Matsu shrugged. "I am here to serve my Emperor."

"No personal feelings?"

"I dislike thieves," Matsu said, "and traitors . . . but who does not? Other than that, no, no personal feelings at all."

Clint thought about that for a while, then poured them each another cup of coffee.

"Why did you ask that?" Matsu asked, eventually.

"About your personal feelings?"

"Yes."

"I don't know. It just seemed to me that you were so single-minded in your pursuit of the thieves that there must be some sort of . . . personal grudge."

"No," Matsu said, "no . . . grudge. I am simply loyal to my Emperor."

"I see," Clint said.

"And understand?"

Clint hesitated. "I think so. On occasion I have been . . . called to serve my country." He was thinking of the times that his friend, Jim West, who was an agent for the American Secret Service, would draft him into the service as well—temporarily. Although he had accepted these jobs at first as a favor to West, in the end he had realized that he was also serving his government. For this reason, Clint never refused West's requests. "It's sometimes necessary to act out of sheer loyalty, I know that."

"Yes," Matsu said, "I can see that you do . . . but . . ."

"But what?"

Matsu stared into the darkness. Both men avoided looking directly into the fire, to preserve their night vision.

"I am not above having personal feelings."

"Oh? Against who?"

"The man Lee."

"Oh," Clint said, nodding his head. "When we get back we'll have to talk to him."

"I do not want to *talk*."

"Matsu, we're going to have to give him a chance to explain—"

"You give him a chance to explain," Matsu said. "I know that he sent us into a trap, to be killed. For that I *will* have vengeance."

Clint sat back with his coffee and regarded Matsu across the fire. The man's face was sternly set, as it usually was. It remained the same whether he was talking about his Emperor's justice or his own vengeance. It was only by the feverish glow in his eyes when he spoke of Lee that Clint could see how strongly he felt about the man.

Clint dropped the subject. "We'll take turns sleeping and standing watch," he said.

"Yes."

"I'll stand watch first."

"No," Matsu said, "I will stand watch first. You get some sleep. I am not sleepy."

"Well, I am," Clint said, "so I won't argue with you."

Clint rolled himself up in his blanket. Before going to sleep he asked Matsu, "Do you want my rifle?"

"No," Matsu said, "my own weapons will serve."

"Have it your way," Clint said. "Give a holler if anything happens."

FORTY-ONE

The night passed uneventfully. Matsu woke Clint for his watch, during which he made himself another pot of coffee. Once he went over to check the horses and talk to Duke for a little while. Basically he apologized for all the time the big gelding had had to spend in the San Francisco livery stable. He promised the big horse that when this was over they'd get on the trail again.

Just before the sun peaked above the horizon Clint turned to wake Matsu, but the man stirred and rose on his own.

"Time to get going," Clint said. "Want some coffee before we start?"

"No," Matsu said, standing up. "I am ready to go now."

Clint admired the way the man did not seem to have to work any kinks out of his body after sleeping on the ground. Clint, though he was used to sleeping on the ground, usually had to stretch for a few minutes to loosen up his muscles.

Clint doused the fire and packed away their

coffee pot. They saddled their own horses and mounted up.

"Which way?" Matsu asked.

"There," Clint said, pointing east.

"Will we get there today?" Matsu asked as they started to ride.

"If we push," Clint said, "we can get there by nightfall. I figure they'll probably be there by midday. If we scared Gaines enough he won't send a telegram, and they won't know we're coming."

"They will know I am coming," Matsu said.

"How?"

He turned and looked at Clint.

"They knew all along I would come after them," the Japanese warrior said. "They will be expecting me."

"Great," Clint said. "I guess we can kiss our element of surprise good-bye, right?"

"It does not matter," Matsu replied. "Whether they know we are coming or not, they will die."

"There's something we should discuss, Matsu," Clint said.

"What?"

"Your Emperor's justice," Clint answered. "Will it extend beyond the two thieves?"

"What do you mean?"

"I mean," Clint said, "will your Emperor expect you to kill the man whose only crime is buying the sword? I'm talking about this Henderson Burke."

"No," Matsu said, "I have no obligation to kill him."

"Well, good," Clint said, "because if he's as

wealthy as Gaines indicated, that would be a little hard to explain."

"To who?"

"To the law."

Matsu looked straight ahead. "We will not break your country's law."

"No," Clint said, "we'll just take the sword and kill two men, that's all."

"Correct," Matsu agreed, failing to see the humor in the remark. "That is all."

As they rode along in silence Clint couldn't help but wish they'd had a little more time to plan this. For one thing, he would have liked to look up this Henderson Burke and get some information on the man. As a wealthy rancher he was sure to have a large force of men on his property. How was he going to feel and react to Toshiro Matsu trying to retrieve the sword for the Emperor, its rightful owner? Surely Burke must have known that such a sword was stolen when he agreed to purchase it. If he didn't care about that, then maybe he wouldn't care to just stand by and allow its return.

Questions, he thought, all questions that would eventually be answered when they got there—and probably answered the hard way.

FORTY-TWO

Henderson Burke looked down at the gleaming metal of the Emperor's Sword and couldn't believe his luck. This would be the crowning achievement, the jewel of his weapons collection.

"It's breathtaking," he said.

The sword lay on his desk. He stood behind the desk, and in front of it stood the two Japanese he was sure had stolen the sword. With them were the three men Daryl Gaines had provided to guide them to the Bar-HB ranch. Also in the room were Burke's foreman, Carl Wilcox, and three of his men.

"What do you need them for?" one of Gaines's men had asked as they all entered the house. His name was Jacks, and he was referring to Wilcox and the other three men.

"The boss don't go nowhere without being covered," Wilcox had said.

"Not even his own house?" Jacks had asked.

"That's right," Wilcox had answered, "not even his own house."

The man had shrugged and said, "I wish I had enough money to buy *that* kind of protection."

Now Burke said again, "It's beautiful."

"We want money," one of the Japanese said. The other simply nodded.

Without looking up from the sword Henderson Burke said, "You'll get your money, gentlemen. Just be patient."

"Not patient," the first Japanese said. "Want money."

"He's the only one who savvies English," Jacks said. "The other only talks that Japanese gibberish."

"Gibberish to us, not to them, I'm sure," Burke said. Again, when he spoke he did not look up from the sword. "Magnificent. I'm sure your Emperor misses it."

"Emperor will send someone for it," the Japanese spokesman said. "Want money so we can get away."

Now Burke looked up at the man.

"He'd actually send someone all the way over here to retrieve this?"

"Yes."

"And what about you?"

The Japanese frowned.

"Will he want you back, also?"

"No," the man said, "we will be kill. Need money to run."

"Well," Burke said, "with the amount of money I agreed to pay, you could run a long way."

"Hey," Jacks said, "don't forget about us. We got to take some money back to our boss."

"Yes, yes," Burke said, impatiently, "you will all get what is coming to you, don't worry. Just let me . . . let me *look* at it."

"You pay," the Japanese said, "then you look."

With that he stepped forward and reached for the sword. On the wall behind Burke besides a window there were many bladed weapons hanging, knives and swords of varying sizes and shapes. As the Japanese reached for the Emperor's Sword Burke reached behind him, plucked a dueling sword from the wall and in one swift motion drove the blade into the chest of the Japanese. The man's mouth opened, but no sound came out. His eyes popped, and as Burke pulled the slender weapon free the man slumped to the floor, dead.

The other Japanese started to talk very rapidly in his own language.

"Yes," Burke said, speaking to no one in particular, "it does sound like gibberish, doesn't it?"

With a flick of his eyes he gave a silent order to his foreman, who stepped forward, produced a knife from his belt, grabbed the hair of the remaining Japanese, pulled on it so that his throat was well exposed, and then slit his throat.

"Put them over there, on the throw rug," Burke said. "We can wrap them in it so they don't bleed on the floor."

Too stunned to speak up to that point, Gaines's man suddenly said, "Shit!"

He went for his gun, as did his partners, but they were quickly grabbed from behind by Burke's men, held fast and disarmed.

"Jesus," Jacks said, staring at Burke, "you gonna kill us, too, rather than pay what you owe?"

"It was not my intention to kill anyone," Burke said. He placed the dueling sword back on the wall without cleaning it off. "That is, until *that* heathen tried to take my sword—and it *is* my sword, gentlemen."

"Yeah, sure," Jacks said, nervously, "of course it's your sword."

"You don't dispute that?"

"No, no, of course not," Jacks said. "Why would I?"

"And you men?" Burke said to the others.

They shook their heads and said no, they didn't dispute it.

"Very well," Burke said. "Do any of you object to what has happened to these two heathens?"

"Hell, no," Jacks said, forcing a grin, "we didn't like them, anyway. L-look, Mr. Burke, if you just let us go—"

"Without payment?"

"Hell, you don't wanna pay, don't pay," Jacks said. "Let Mr. Gaines take it up with you."

"And what will you tell Mr. Gaines?"

"We don't gotta tell him nothing," Jacks said. "Hell, we don't even have to go back to San Francisco, you know?"

"Yes," Burke said, "I know." He looked at his foreman and said, "Pay them off and let them go."

"Yessir."

Burke took a fat envelope from a desk drawer and tossed it to Wilcox.

"Take them outside," Wilcox told his men. "We'll pay them out there."

As Gaines's men were hustled from the room Wilcox looked back at his boss, who nodded to him. Before leaving the room Wilcox placed the envelope of money back on the desk.

Burke's feeling was that he had just saved himself the amount of money that would have gone to the Japanese, and if he had given Gaines's money to those three men, they probably would have stolen it. No, he'd send Gaines a bank draft for his commission, and explain that his men had been killed by the two Japanese, who in turn were killed by Burke's men. Unfortunate, and tragic, but then Burke would have the sword, and Gaines would have his commission—and Henderson Burke would have saved himself the remainder of the purchase price.

It was the only way to do business.

FORTY-THREE

In spite of the fact that Matsu's Morgan couldn't quite keep pace with Duke, they made pretty good time. In fact, Clint felt that his prediction of reaching the ranch—or, at least, Stone City—by nightfall was within their grasp.

Finally, Clint reined Duke in and waited for Matsu to catch up.

"You do not have to keep waiting for me to catch up," Matsu said. "I will not lose you."

"I wasn't waiting for you to catch up," Clint said. He pointed. "There's Stone City."

Matsu looked ahead in the direction Clint was pointing. Stone City sprawled out ahead of them. It did not look like a city to him, however, since he was comparing the place to San Francisco.

"It is small," he said.

"But growing," Clint said, "probably due in part to Henderson Burke. The town probably owes a lot of its prosperity to him and his ranch."

Matsu looked at Clint and said, "You are trying to tell me something."

"Yes," Clint said. "I think we'd better bypass

the town. We won't find any help there, especially if Burke doesn't *want* to let the sword go. I mean, if we have to *take* it from him, that town is no place for us to be."

"So we go right to the ranch."

"Yes."

Matsu looked at the sky. "It will be dark soon."

"We'll find it," Clint said. "In fact, I think we're better off approaching it in the dark. We may have to take back this sword in the dark."

"I will do it," Matsu said, "day or night."

"Let me ask you something else, here."

"No."

"No?"

"No," Matsu said. "I will not settle for the sword and let the thieves go."

Clint stared at him, then asked, "What are you, some kind of a mind reader?"

"I do not have to read your mind," Matsu said. "I know you would rather take the sword without further bloodshed."

"Is that bad?"

"I also know," Matsu said, "that if it does come to bloodshed I can be confident fighting by your side."

"I'll fight with you, Matsu," Clint said, "if there's no other way. You can count on that."

"I know that."

"Hopefully," Clint added, "there *will* be another way."

Matsu didn't reply.

"Come on," Clint said, with a sigh, "we'll go around the town this way."

FORTY-FOUR

It was dark by the time they came within sight of the ranch.

"Let's leave the horses here," Clint said.

"I do not understand," Matsu said. "Why do we not just ride in and tell this man that we have come for the sword."

"And you think he's going to just give it to you?" Clint asked.

"I am the emissary of the rightful owner," Matsu said.

"That doesn't matter to someone who buys stolen items, Matsu," Clint said.

"Perhaps he does not know it is stolen."

"He knows," Clint said.

"Still," Matsu said, "I must give him a chance to give it back before we do anything else."

"What about your two countrymen?"

"They will die, no matter what," Matsu said, "but I will not go against this other man if he is willing to give the sword back."

"All right," Clint said, "but we're still going to have to move quietly. Once we get inside we'll give him a chance to give it back."

"Then why must we move in the darkness, on foot?" Matsu asked.

"Trust me on this, Matsu," Clint said. "Once we get into the house, then you can talk to him the way you want to."

Matsu still looked puzzled, but he said he would follow Clint.

The main house was lit up, as was the bunkhouse. Clint and Matsu came from the direction of the huge barn, with the main house between them and the bunkhouse. They had a good chance of getting to the house without raising the alarm.

They had reached the barn on foot when the door of the bunkhouse opened.

"Inside," Clint said, and they ducked into the barn quickly.

A couple of hands came out of the bunkhouse and started towards the barn.

"We've got to hide ourselves," Clint said. "They're coming this way."

They both found places to secret themselves: Matsu in an empty stall and Clint behind a pile of hay.

As the men approached they could hear that they were having an argument.

" . . . this is dumb," one man was saying. "We can't race in the dark."

"Look," the other man said, "you claim your horse is faster than mine. I want to prove that you're wrong."

"In the dark?" the other man said. "Come on, by the time we get back all the whiskey will be gone. We can race tomorrow, when it's light."

"Okay," the second man said, "and then every-one can watch."

"Right," the first man said.

They stopped short of entering the barn, turned and went back to the bunkhouse.

"Matsu," Clint said, coming out from behind the pile of hay. "Matsu."

"I am here," Matsu said.

"Well, come on—"

"You should come here," Matsu said. He stepped out of the stall and waved to Clint, who could barely make him out. "Over here."

Clint walked over to join Matsu, who gestured toward the stall. It took a moment for Clint's eyes to adjust, but he thought he saw . . . bodies.

"Jesus," Clint said. "How many?"

"Five," Matsu said.

"Who are they?"

"The thieves I was seeking," Matsu said, "and three of your countrymen."

"Gaines's men," Clint said. "Are they all dead?"

"Yes."

"Burke," Clint said. "He didn't have any inten-tion of paying for the sword." He turned to look at Matsu and added, "And this is the man you think is going to just give the sword back?"

"Obviously," Matsu said, "I am wrong."

"Obviously," Clint said. He looked back into the stall. "Well, at least this part was done for you. Now all we need to do is recover the sword."

"Yes."

"We can just sneak into the house and take it," Clint said. "There's no need to confront *anyone*."

It was odd, he thought, but the death of five men had worked to their advantage. They might be able to get out of this without actually engaging anyone.

That is, if the sword was somewhere in plain sight.

"Let's get to the house," Clint said.

"Should we not wait until the house is dark?" Matsu asked.

"No," Clint said, "let's go and see what we can see in the light. Once we locate the sword, we can go and get it in the dark with no problem."

Matsu nodded his agreement, and they started for the house.

FORTY-FIVE

As they neared the house Clint and Matsu saw that it was the right side that was lit up. They were approaching the house from the left, so they circled completely around it in order not to cross in front of it. When they reached the right side they flattened themselves against the wall, taking advantage of the shadows. Luckily, anyone coming out of the bunkhouse would be coming from the light into the dark, and it would take some time for his eyes to adjust to the darkness.

They moved along the side of the house, Matsu behind Clint. Clint put up his hand for Matsu to stop and leaned over to look in a window. It looked like a sitting room or a library. There was a desk with a burning lamp on it, but there was no one there, and there was no sign of any sword. If Burke collected the damned things there should have been something in view.

Clint ducked as he went by the window, and Matsu followed his example.

They came to another lighted window and Clint repeated his actions. This time he was rewarded. The desk was right in front of the window. If someone had been sitting at it, Clint would have been looking at the back of his head.

This room was different. Although it had a desk, there were no books. Instead, there were all sorts of bladed weapons on the wall— and on the desk was a magnificent, gleaming sword.

Clint backed away from the window and asked Matsu, "Is that it?"

Matsu moved past him, looked in the window, then turned and said, "That is it." There was almost a hint of repressed excitement in his voice. It was the most excited Clint had ever seen the man get.

"We must get inside," Matsu said.

Clint shrugged and said, "Try the window."

Matsu tried the window, and it was open.

"Burke must be pretty damn sure of his security," Clint said. "Let's go inside."

Matsu opened the window wide enough for them to climb inside, which they did. Matsu went immediately to the sword. He did not pick it up, but ran his finger along the blade.

"Is it not beautiful?" he said.

Clint stood next to him and looked down at the weapon. The blade gleamed, and there were etchings all along it. The hilt was plain, but it was so black and polished that Clint could see himself in it.

"It sure is," he agreed.

"Yes, gentlemen," someone said, entering the room, "it is quite exquisite, which is why I purchased it."

A man Clint assumed was Henderson Burke entered the room. He was a small, pot-bellied man with white hair. Behind him stood a taller man, who stepped into the room and moved to his right. Some more men came in behind him, six or seven of them, fanning out as they entered. Clint was going to draw his gun when he sensed danger from behind. He took a look. Two men were leaning in the window with their guns already out.

"A trap," Clint said.

"Oh, yes," Burke said.

"You going to kill us like those poor devils in the barn?"

"Yes, indeed," Burke said, "and we'll probably bury you all in the same deep hole."

"Do you want to know why we're here?"

"I already know," Burke said. "This interesting looking gentleman with you is no doubt from Japan, here at the behest of the Emperor to retrieve his sword."

"That's right."

"Well," Burke said, "he can't have it back. It's mine, now."

"No!" Matsu shouted. He turned and before anyone could move, his sword lashed out and sliced off the hands of both men leaning in the window. They started to scream as their blood shot across the desk to the other end of the room.

Matsu moved again, and two *shuriken* sailed across the room, striking two of Burke's men.

Clint moved quickly, dropping to his knees and grabbing one of the fallen guns. He had to pry the severed hand from it in order to use it.

By this time Matsu had literally sprung over the desk, surprising the remaining men. Clint came up with the gun and began to fire as quickly as he could thumb back the hammer on the single-action Colt.

Matsu was slashing with his sword and men were screaming and squeezing the triggers of their guns. The gun in Clint's hand was suddenly empty, and he tossed it aside and picked up the Emperor's Sword. In a split second he was side by side with Matsu, and their blades were flashing and hacking.

Clint swung the unfamiliar blade and buried it in the foreman's shoulder. He screamed and went down to his knees, and in that moment Clint saw Henderson Burke run from the room.

He looked around and there was no one standing but he and Matsu.

"Check them all," Clint called out. "I'll get Henderson."

"Hai!!" Matsu said.

Clint ran out of the room, looked up and down the hall, then heard something to his left. He ran that way and saw a lamp lying smashed on the floor. In his haste Burke had knocked it over. Clint continued on and found himself in a large living room. Henderson Burke was reaching over the fireplace for an army saber that was hanging there. He turned with it in his hand.

"Now," he said, his eyes gleaming, "show me the Emperor's Sword in action . . ."

The little man stood with his feet spread and the saber held out in front of him. His balance looked good, and Clint had no doubt that, although he presented a comical sight, he knew how to use the saber. A sword was not Clint's weapon of choice; he knew he was at a disadvantage.

"Put it down, Burke," Clint said. He dropped his blade down by his side. "It's all over."

"I want that sword," Burke said.

"This one?" Clint asked, jiggling the Emperor's Sword down along his leg. "You can't have it. It's the property of the Japanese government."

"You can't prove that."

"I don't have to," Clint said. "I have the sword."

"I'll—I'll come over there and get it."

At that point they were joined in the room by Matsu. Clint turned and Matsu tossed him his gun. Clint, in turn, handed the Emperor's Sword over to the Japanese warrior.

"Okay," he said, holstering his gun and looking at Burke, "*now* it's over."

Burke's face filled, turning red, and then he shouted and charged Clint like he thought he was a Japanese warrior. Before he could reach his prey, however, Matsu was between them. His sword rose and fell, and when he moved out of the way Clint could see Burke, cleaved from throat to crotch, as he fell over.

"Okay," Clint said to no one in particular, "*now* it's over."

FORTY-SIX

Clint and Matsu retraced the steps they had taken the first time they went to see Nok Woo Lee. The Emperor's Sword was safe. They had returned with it the day before and now all that remained was to settle accounts with Lee.

For some reason Clint felt sure that the man would answer his door and let them in, which he did. Lee did not strike Clint as the kind of man to hide. Then again, he hadn't struck him as a dishonorable man, either, but to take their money to do a job and then set them up to be killed was as dishonorable as you could get.

Not that Clint put as much stock in honor as Toshiro Matsu appeared to. For one thing, it did not strike Clint that killing should be done in the name of honor, but he knew that was what Matsu had in mind.

"Come in, gentlemen," Lee said.

He led them to his quarters, where they had

met previously, and then turned to face them.

"What can I do for you?"

"I think you know," Clint said. "Aren't you surprised to see us alive?"

"Frankly," Lee said, "yes."

"You took money, Lee, from us," Clint said, "and then from Gaines to send us into a trap."

"Actually," Lee said, "I took the money from Ballard, but no matter. It was, after all, Gaines's money."

"What do you have to say for yourself?"

Lee shrugged.

"A man must make a living."

"You have no honor," Matsu said.

Lee looked at Matsu calmly and asked, "And what do you intend to do about it?"

"Since you cannot live with honor," Matsu said, "I will teach you how to die with it."

"With your sword?" Lee asked. "Or are you man enough to face me without it."

This was the confrontation that Clint had not wanted to see. Of course, that was *before* he realized that Lee had sent them into a trap.

"I do not need my sword," Matsu said. He removed it and handed it to Clint.

"And what about you?" Lee asked, removing his pajama-type clothing. Beneath it he wore some kind of loincloth. He was not muscular, but Clint could see that his slender body was hard.

"This is a matter of honor," Clint said, "between you and him."

"And if I kill him you'll turn around and leave?" Lee asked.

"Yes," Clint said, "until another time."

"So be it," Lee said.

Clint stepped back and privately wondered if he would be able to stay out of the battle if it looked like Matsu was about to be killed.

"It is a matter of honor," Matsu had said to him earlier. "You must not interfere, no matter what."

"Not even to save your life?"

"It is better to die with honor," Matsu had said, "than to live without it."

Clint had shaken his head and said, "We have very different philosophies, my friend."

Now as the two combatants circled each other he knew that, no matter what he saw, he *had* to stay out of it, even if it meant Matsu would die. Also, if that happened, he would *have* to turn and walk out, or be a man without honor, himself.

He had no doubt that Lee would let him walk out if that were the case, and that they would meet again at a later date.

There was a brief flurry of activity as each man darted in and out, testing the other's speed and reactions. Matsu was the bigger man, but Clint thought that Lee might be the faster of the two. If this were a boxing ring, Clint would naturally go with the bigger man. It was his experience that a good big man could always beat a good little man. As he continued to watch he found it much less interesting than a boxing match.

Lee seemed to be the only one landing blows, but for all intents and purposes they appeared not to affect Matsu. Lee had the speed to get in and out, but he didn't have the power to hurt Matsu.

After a half hour of feinting and jabbing by Lee, the American/Chinese finally made an error. Out of frustration at not being able to hurt the bigger Japanese man he got too close, and underestimated Matsu's speed. Before Lee knew it— and Clint—Matsu closed his arms around the man. Before long Matsu had Lee on his back, across one knee and helpless. He bent the smaller man back . . . back . . . back until Clint heard an audible *crack* . . . and Lee went totally limp.

Matsu rolled the dead man off his knee onto the floor, walked over to Clint and accepted his sword back.

"Not enough size," Clint said.

"Now he has honor," Matsu said as the two men left.

Outside Clint shook his head once again. "I just don't see how killing can bring honor, Matsu. I'll *never* understand it."

"You do not have to," Matsu said.

They started back to the hotel.

"When will you be leaving?"

"Tomorrow," Matsu said.

"I hope . . . ," Clint started, and then stopped.

"What?" Matsu asked.

Clint turned to face the man.

"I hope that even though our philosophies are

different, that we will be parting as friends."

Matsu didn't hesitate. He put his hand out and the two men clasped hands warmly and with respect.

"Yes," Matsu said, "we are friends."

Watch for

GAMBLER'S BLOOD

141st novel in the exciting GUNSMITH series
from Jove

Coming in September!

J. R. ROBERTS

THE

GUNSMITH